MIRROR OF LIFE

BY

NAJIBA DARWISH KAKAR

Dedication

With all the essence of my being, I dedicate this book…

To all the women who screamed in silence, to the mothers who stayed awake through nights of pain and still greeted the dawn with a smile, to the sisters whose backs bent under the weight of injustice, yet whose hearts stood tall, and to the daughters who were forced to meet sorrow before they ever embraced a doll.

I dedicate this to all those who will find themselves within the lines of these pages;

To the wounded who still manage to smile at life, to the souls who discovered light while walking through darkness, and to every heart still searching for meaning, love, and peace.

Above all,

I dedicate this to my lost self—

Who stood again after being shattered by pain, exile, loneliness, and migration; who gathered her broken pieces, wrote again, and breathed hope back into life.

This book is a mirror for every soul that has once been broken—

And yet, with its shattered pieces, became a light for others.

With all my love,

Najiba Darwish

Mirror of Life

Foreword: The Voice of Wounds, the Whisper of Hope

This book is for those who have remained silent.

For hearts that have endured pain but had no place to speak of it.

For tears shed in the darkness of night, unseen by anyone.

And for smiles that hid entire worlds of breaking inside.

If you've ever felt like you're falling behind in life…

If you've ever wished that, just for a moment, someone would truly see you…

If you've ever wondered: "Is it just me who feels this way?"

Know this—this book is reaching out to you. No judgment, no advice, no ready-made solutions.

There are no quick fixes here. No motivational clichés.

We simply walk together.

We sit side by side, we talk, we stay silent, maybe cry…

And slowly, without even noticing, we begin to breathe again.

We begin to feel hope again. To feel life again.

This is a collection of pieces from the heart.

My heart, your heart, the hearts of all those who once broke somewhere along the way…

But still stood up again.

If you're ready, let's walk this path together.

Not toward forgetting the pain, but toward understanding it.

Because only through understanding pain can we find the light that might save us.

From the heart of darkness,

To the light…

Foreword

Life often weaves paths filled with twists and turns, leading us into heartbreak and longing. At every corner of this journey, we face challenges that strike deeply into our minds, our hearts, our very souls. But within these struggles lies a greater truth: every failure, every moment of pain, can be the beginning of inner transformation.

This book, The Mirror of Life, is an attempt to capture those moments of transformation, both silent and overwhelming. As we search for peace and self-understanding amidst the noise of the world, we hold up a mirror that reflects not the outer world, but the depths within. In this mirror, images of pain, hope, loneliness, love, and liberation come to life.

This book speaks of breaking—of those moments when all hope seems lost. Yet, within those moments is the quiet strength to rebuild and return to oneself, changed and stronger than before. This is where we begin to hear silence, and in that silence, we find the voice of our own heart. It's where we meet our inner wounds, and from that encounter, gather the strength to begin again.

The purpose of this book is to remind you: you are not alone on this journey. Every person, carrying their own kind of pain and battle, is in search of peace and freedom. This book is not here to make life seem easier or painless—but to show how, through pain and challenge, we can not only survive, but see life with deeper clarity and meaning.

Truly, isn't there a powerful lesson in every experience? Isn't every mistake also a doorway to transformation? May this book help you see each day, each moment, as a chance to understand yourself more deeply.

Introduction

In a world that moves too fast, we often rush past our feelings. Past the griefs that go unspoken, the joys that are never fully felt, and the fears we're too afraid to face.

This book is not a guide to better living. It is not a prescription for happiness. It is a reflection of what makes us human: vulnerability, pain, love, hope, and the quiet strength to rise again, even after breaking.

The Mirror of Life is the result of years of writing, feeling, and the silent hours born in the depths of night. These are words that have slowly taken shape in solitude, in journeys, in longing, and in the return to oneself.

May each word create meaning for you.

And may each page be an invitation—

to return home to yourself.

Table of Contents

Chapter One: Where Do We Hide When Life Gets Hard?

Instead of an Introduction:

Life is not always kind. Sometimes it pushes us, sometimes it knocks us down, and sometimes it silences us so deeply that we can't even hear our voice.

This chapter is for those moments.

The moments when we smile on the outside, but feel empty within.

When all we want is for someone to just listen, without judging,

Without offering a solution.

Where do we hide?

When life gets hard, we all look for shelter in our own way.

- Some hide in silence.

- Some in prayer.

- Some in quiet midnight tears.

- And some in the arms of someone who simply knows how to listen.

But maybe the most important shelter is within ourselves.

Somewhere deep in our hearts, within the very pain that, despite everything, has kept us alive.

Because pain, if it doesn't break us, builds us.

You are not alone.

You might think no one understands you.

But the truth is, every person you see is fighting a silent battle.

A wound. A loss. A silent cry.

And yet, each of them holds a hidden strength—

A strength that can turn darkness into light.

Today. Right now.

If your heart feels heavy today, know this: you are not alone.

Right now, thousands of other hearts are beating in tune with yours.

And this page, this book, is here to tell you:

You are still here—

And that means, there is still hope.

Looking ahead…

In the chapters to come, we will talk about loneliness, depression, migration, the pain of losing loved ones, and the many silent sorrows of life.

Maybe we won't find all the answers

But together, we will ask the right questions.

And remember:

Even when it's hard… You are not alone.

Chapter Two: Invisible Among People (Extended Version)

Just a Few Steps from Loneliness…

Have you ever been to a party, surrounded by laughter and noise,

But felt like there was a glass wall around you?

You're there… and yet, not really.

You look around, but no one truly sees you.

No one asks, "How are you?"

And you don't answer either.

Because you've learned that people rarely have time to truly listen.

You're Alive… but Not Living

People who seem okay aren't always okay.

People who laugh aren't always happy.

Some of us have been unseen for so long,

we've started to believe maybe… we're not meant to be seen.

And that's the most painful kind of forgetting—

When you slowly start forgetting yourself.

Have You Grown Distant from Yourself?

Maybe you've been so quiet that even your inner voice has gone silent.

Maybe you've worn so many masks that you don't even know how you feel.

Maybe you've been "strong" for so long

that you're just… tired of being strong.

But let me tell you this:

You are still in there.

That same person who once longed to be seen, understood, and loved.

You Have the Right to Exist—Exactly As You Are

You don't have to be "fine" all the time to be accepted.

You don't have to shrink yourself to make space for others.

You, just as you are, are enough.

If no one has truly seen you until now,

It's not your fault.

Some people only see with their eyes, not with their hearts.

But there are hearts out there that can feel you.

Even if they've never met you.

Even if they're miles away.

Hearts that, like yours, have felt lost in the crowd.

And Maybe… We Were Never Truly Alone

If today, you feel invisible—

Know this:

Right now, hundreds, thousands of others feel the same way.

And that means…

We're not invisible.

We're just standing among those who've forgotten how to truly see.

So let's start with us.

Let's see each other—with our hearts, not just our eyes.

I see you.

With all your silence, your weariness, and your quiet hope.

And this book—book-this moment-is—is a place where we can be together.

In being seen.

In being understood.

In simply being human.

Chapter Three: The Sorrows No One Sees

The Quiet Wounds, the Hidden Ache

The Sorrows Without a Name…

There are pains you can't cry about.

You can't even explain them.

Because they have no name.

Because you're not even sure where they came from—

only that they've made a home inside your chest.

They rise at night,

when the world sleeps,

and you're lying awake,

staring at the ceiling,

thinking of the past,

thinking of all the things you never said…

"Are you okay?"

It's the shortest question in the world.

But when you can't answer it,

when you want to say "no" but only smile instead,

that's when sorrow begins to grow—

quietly, but powerfully.

No one knows the weight you carry.

No one sees how tired you are

from pretending to be strong.

No one asks,

"What is it that broke you this deeply?"

The Wound That Doesn't Bleed Hurts the Most

A wound with no blood needs no bandage,

yet it pulses in your soul,

loud enough to silence your days.

These kinds of sorrows are like shadows—

They follow you to work,

into classrooms, into parties, into crowds…

They're always there.

But no one sees them.

And you—

You fight them quietly, alone.

Longings No One Takes Seriously

Maybe you miss a childhood that's long gone.

Maybe you miss the person you once were—

The one full of dreams and fire.

Maybe you ache for a love that was never returned,

or for chances that passed you by,

before you even knew how much they mattered.

These longings—

They're subtle.

Not loud enough to make you cry,

but deep enough to drown you in silence.

So What Do You Do With It All?

The first step:

Let yourself feel it.

You have the right to be sad,

even if you don't know why.

You have the right to feel tired,

even if the world sees you as "strong."

You have the right to go quiet

when you no longer have the energy to explain.

We live in a world that treats sorrow like a weakness.

But sorrow is as real as joy.

And only when we face it, hold it gently,

Can we start to move through it?

The Sorrows No One Saw… Will Be Seen

This chapter is a letter to every soul that broke in silence.

To you, who might be sitting in the dark with your eyes wide open.

To you, who feel something is missing inside,

To you, who feel something missing inside,

but can't quite name it.

Know this:

Here, in these words, you are seen.

Not as a "problem to be fixed,"

But as a whole human—

With all your beauty and all your broken pieces.

And maybe this—

this being seen—

It is the first flicker of light

In all the sorrows, no one ever saw…

Chapter Four: Migration – Longing in a Silent Suitcase

Leaving doesn't always mean arriving.

Sometimes, leaving means tearing a piece from your heart, placing it somewhere far away, and walking past everything you once called "life."

They say migration is building your future elsewhere.

But no one tells you what to do with your memories.

No one asks who you're supposed to share those lonely nights of exile with when the homesickness makes you shiver from within.

The heart doesn't detach from the soil.

When you leave home, only your body moves.

But your heart? It stays behind in a thousand places.

In the morning call to prayer, you used to hear,

In the alley where you walked with friends,

In the smell of bread from the corner bakery,

In your mother's embrace, your father's tea, your sister's voice, your brother's laughter.

Migration means not taking any of that with you.

It means becoming alone. Deeply alone.

Your tongue becomes foreign.

In the new land, you learn a new language.

But you don't know how to say "longing" in it.

Or how to say, "My home was my heart, and now it's empty…"

Every time someone asks, "Where are you from?"

You have a thousand answers, but only say one name.

You don't say it's no longer safe there.

You don't say you're from a place that, despite the wounds, you still love.

Your suitcase is full of things… yet it feels heavy.

It may carry clothes, a few books, or photos.

But what truly weighs it down isn't the objects—

It's the longing.

The memories.

The gaze you no longer see.

And the words that were left unsaid, with no chance now to be spoken.

Exile breaks you quietly.

It doesn't scream.

It slowly silences you from the inside.

People look at you, but they don't see that every night, you talk to yourself, to the walls, to your mother's photo, to a sky that feels unfamiliar.

You learn to smile.

You learn to look strong.

But no one knows that a smile is not from the heart.

Home?

Home is not just walls and a roof.

Home is a scent you recognize.

It's where your heart feels at ease, no matter how small or simple.

When you migrate, you lose your home…

Not just the place, but the feeling of being home.

And rebuilding that feeling in a foreign land

takes time.

It takes tears.

It takes patience.

But still… You came.

You're here.

With all your weariness and longing,

With all your unspoken words,

You still breathe, you still walk,

And you try not to lose yourself.

And that… is courage.

This chapter is for you.

For all the travelers whose hearts still carry the scent of their homeland.

For you who know: migration always leaves a part of you behind…

Yet you continue forward.

You are not alone.

In this book, your heart will be heard.

In your own language.

With your own pain.

With a silence that is no longer quiet.

Chapter Five: Loneliness – When Even You Don't Know Yourself

Loneliness is not always about the absence of others.

Sometimes, it's about the absence of yourself.

When night falls, the lights go out, and you sit in a room

that, despite its silence, is filled with noise—

The noise of thoughts that won't leave you alone,

The noise of memories you want to forget but can't.

Where are you? Your self?

Maybe you've looked into the mirror and asked,

"Is this really me? Why do I look so tired? So faded?"

When loneliness stretches on too long,

you begin to forget your own reflection.

And that's the hardest kind of loneliness—

When you feel like a stranger to yourself.

There are people… but no one really listens

Maybe you have hundreds of contacts in your phone,

Maybe you go to parties, you smile, you joke…

But your heart still feels silent.

Why? Because there's no one who really understands.

Loneliness isn't about being physically alone.

It's having something in your heart

that you can't share with anyone.

You miss yourself

You miss the you you used to be.

The days when you could laugh freely.

The moments when life was hard, but at least it was familiar.

Maybe you feel like you've vanished.

But no… you're still there.

Just hidden under layers of exhaustion, fear, and pretending.

Why can't we talk?

Because we're afraid.

Afraid of being judged.

Afraid they'll say, "Here we go again, always sad."

But what's wrong with that?

There's no shame in sadness.

Silence only makes the pain louder.

What's the first step?

Be gentle with yourself.

Accept that loneliness exists,

But you are not trapped in it.

If you listen to your inner voice,

If you sit beside yourself instead of running away,

Slowly, the darkness begins to lift.

And then maybe,

you'll find yourself again.

You are not alone

If you're reading these words,

know this: you are not alone.

All of us, at some point in life,

have tasted this kind of loneliness.

And this chapter is for you

For every silent night you cried,

For every moment you wished someone would just ask: "How are you?"

And actually wait for your answer.

Chapter Six: Depression – The Days When You Don't Know Why You're Alive

Depression isn't just about feeling sad.

It's about going quiet.

It's seeing a world full of color, but feeling it all in gray.

It's waking up with a heart that finds no reason to keep going.

People with depression are often the best at hiding it.

They smile, they greet others, they go to work—

but inside, the sound of life is gone.

Everything plays like a black-and-white movie.

You exist… but you don't feel like you're living.

Mornings that feel heavy.

You wake up, but don't want to move.

Not because you're lazy—

but because nothing feels worth the effort anymore.

Your tea goes cold.

The laundry piles up.

Messages stay unread.

And you sit there…

not really looking at anything, just staring at the wall.

When you feel like there's no reason to be

Depression creeps in slowly.

So slowly, you don't even notice.

Until one day you ask yourself,

"Why don't I laugh anymore?"

"Why does everything feel so empty?"

Maybe you whisper to yourself,

"What's the point of being here?

Does anyone even notice if I'm gone?"

That moment—

when even crying feels pointless—

It is the loneliest of all.

What does it mean to be "strong"?

We're taught to be strong means to stay quiet.

To push through. To endure without complaining.

But sometimes the bravest thing you can do

is to say, "I'm tired."

"I need help."

If you're feeling like this today,

know this: you are not alone.

What you're feeling is not who you are.

It's just a storm—

Not your identity.

You're not broken. You're wounded.

Depression isn't just something to "fix" with medicine.

It's a silent wound—

One that needs to be felt, seen, and heard.

And sometimes, being seen

is the first step toward healing.

There is a way through… even if you can't see it now

Even in the deepest darkness,

there is still a flicker of light—

Even if you can't see it yet.

This book is a whisper,

a soft reminder:

You made it to this page,

and that means you're still here.

If all you did today was breathe,

if all you could do was stay alive,

that's enough.

You're still here, so there's still hope

We believe this:

Even from these shadowed days,

a sunrise will come.

Not suddenly.

Not easily.

But surely.

So if you feel numb, lost, or tired—

Know this: You're still here.

And that means the story isn't over yet.

Chapter Seven: Loss – The Grief That Stays Inside Us

Death is not the end.

It's a silence that never fully goes away.

It's an empty chair at the table,

A phone number that no longer rings,

A familiar voice that only returns in dreams.

Losing someone you love

feels like falling into a bottomless pit

No one truly understands,

and no one can really help.

People say, "Be patient," or "Time heals everything."

But some wounds… even time grows tired trying to touch them.

Each person who leaves takes a piece of us with them

When you lose someone,

you don't just lose them—

You lose part of yourself.

You were a certain version of yourself with them.

When they're gone, that version fades.

You change. You break—quietly, invisibly.

Grief has a shape… but no words

The sorrow of death has no clear language.

You can't fully describe it.

Because it's made of so many things—

Longing. Anger. Confusion.

And sometimes… complete numbness.

You might feel pressure to be "strong."

To hide the tears. To stay composed.

But why?

Who said grief is weakness?

You have every right to break

If today you cried,

if you heard their voice in your mind and your heart trembled,

if you sat at the dinner table and noticed their absence like a wound—

know that it only means you loved deeply.

And it means you're alive.

You still feel. You still carry love.

And that… is the most human thing there is.

We don't forget—but we learn to live with the sorrow

You won't forget someone who meant the world to you.

But you can learn to live beside the ache.

Not like before

but with respect for the memories,

With a soft kiss to their photo,

With a bittersweet smile at the moments you once shared.

They're gone… but you're still here

And your life now…

It is a continuation of theirs.

Every time you show kindness,

every time you love,

they live on—

not in body,

but in meaning.

In memory.

In the heart.

And if today you just missed them…

That's enough.

That alone says: the bond is still there, even beyond death.

And that bond…

It might just be the thing that pulls you back to life

Slowly. Quietly. But surely.

Chapter Eight: Who said grief is weakness?

You have every right to break

If today you cried,

if you heard their voice in your mind and your heart trembled,

if you sat at the dinner table and noticed their absence like a wound—

know that it only means you loved deeply.

And it means you're alive.

You still feel. You still carry love.

And that… is the most human thing there is.

We don't forget—but we learn to live with the sorrow

You won't forget someone who meant the world to you.

But you can learn to live beside the ache.

Not like before

but with respect for the memories,

With a soft kiss to their photo,

With a bittersweet smile at the moments you once shared.

They're gone… but you're still here

And your life now…

is a continuation of theirs.

Every time you show kindness,

every time you love,

they live on—

not in body,

but in meaning.

In memory.

In the heart.

And if today you just missed them…

That's enough.

That alone says: the bond is still there, even beyond death.

And that bond…

It might just be the thing that pulls you back to life

Slowly. Quietly. But surely.

But you haven't let go.

And that means you're strong.

Not in the way the world defines strength,

but in your own quiet, steady, unseen way.

Migration is a wound that slowly forms a new skin

One day, you begin returning to yourself.

Not to the physical house,

but to a place inside you

a home no one can take from you.

And when that day comes,

your heart finds peace.

Najiba Darwish Kakar

Not because you no longer miss anything,

but because you've made peace with missing.

Chapter Nine: Returning to Yourself – When the Path Leads Inward

Sometimes, in trying so hard to please others,

chasing after all the "shoulds" and "musts,"

and getting lost in the noise of the world,

we forget who we were.

We forget why we even started…

And one day, we open our eyes and realize:

We're no longer the person we used to be.

And the road we're on?

It no longer feels like ours.

When everything falls apart…

Maybe right now, you're standing in that place—

exhausted from pretending,

tired of carrying pain in silence,

weary of fake smiles and empty motivation.

No hope. No drive. Just… emptiness.

But right there—yes, right there—

where it feels like the end,

could actually be the beginning.

The beginning of your return.

Not to the past,

but to yourself.

Your true self isn't lost—it's just quiet

In the silence within you now,

beneath all the pain and the breaking,

there's a voice.

A gentle one.

Maybe it's been quiet for years.

But it's still there.

And it's waiting…

for you to be quiet enough to hear it again.

Returning to yourself means making peace with your flaws.

It means accepting that you're not perfect—

that you fall sometimes,

you're afraid sometimes,

you even get tired of yourself.

But still, you hold yourself gently.

Like a mother holding her child—

not because the child is flawless,

but because love doesn't ask for perfection.

You are enough… exactly as you are

You don't need to be more, or better, or stronger.

The fact that you're still here, still breathing,

still surviving your storms—

means you are enough.

The fact that you're willing to find your way back to yourself

means there is still light—

even in your darkest hour.

When the outside world fails to lead you anywhere, it's time to go inward

Return to your heart.

To the words you never said.

To the dreams you left somewhere in childhood.

To you.

And don't forget—

No one can save you more powerfully than you can.

Everything begins here…

from within.

Chapter Ten: Forgiveness – Breaking Free from the Chains of the Past

Sometimes the pain runs so deep, even thinking about forgiveness makes your heart tremble.

You whisper to yourself:

"How can I forgive someone who broke me?

Who silenced my voice?

Who turned my dreams into nightmares?"

But here's the truth…

Forgiveness doesn't mean forgetting.

No—you may never forget that word, that look, that dark night.

But you can choose not to relive it—

not every day, not every moment, not anymore.

We carry pain like a shadow behind us

Each of us has a wound we hide behind a smile.

Some wounds trace back to childhood.

Some are carved by the betrayal of those we trusted most.

Some are born from within—

from the choices we made… or didn't make.

And unless we tend to those wounds,

they grow into chains.

Heavy, silent… but suffocating.

Why forgive?

Not to be the "bigger person."

Not to earn someone's approval.

But because… you're tired.

Tired of carrying pain like a second skin.

Forgiveness means understanding this:

The past cannot be undone—

But the present can be healed,

and the future can still be yours.

Forgiving yourself is the hardest part

Sometimes, it's not others.

It's you you can't forgive.

For the mistakes you made.

The moments you stayed silent when you should have spoken.

The love you gave was never returned.

But believe me:

If you don't forgive yourself,

you'll stay locked inside a prison you built with your own hands.

And you deserve freedom.

Forgiveness is a journey, not a moment

Maybe today, you can't forgive.

That's okay.

Maybe your heart is still too heavy.

That's okay too.

Just wanting to forgive is the first step.

That tiny desire is already movement—

toward light, toward healing.

And in the end…

Forgive.

With tears, with a shaking voice, with a trembling heart—but still, forgive.

Choose forgiveness, not because it's easy—

But because you deserve to live without open wounds.

Forgive,

and see how slowly…

Your breath softens,

your eyes rest easier at night,

and your heart begins to beat—just a little more freely.

Chapter Eleven: Loneliness – The Quiet Voice Within

Sometimes silence is the loudest sound you hear.

Not from the outside—but from within.

When everyone leaves,

when your phone stays quiet,

when you look in the mirror and only see tired eyes staring back…

That's when loneliness shows itself.

Loneliness is frightening, yes.

But it is not our enemy.

It is like a night that comes after all the noise,

to bring you face-to-face with yourself.

Have you ever truly seen yourself?

Not the version you created for others.

Not the half-smile or the rehearsed answers.

The real you—

With all the pain, the hope, the fears,

and the unfinished dreams.

Loneliness comes to remind you:

There is a voice inside—soft but deep—

One you often ignore.

A voice that says,

"I'm still here. I'm still alive. I still want to live."

You can run from loneliness.

With noise. With meaningless relationships. With overwork.

With anything.

But eventually,

in some moment,

in some place,

you'll meet it again.

And when you do—if you're brave—

You'll realize loneliness is not an empty space.

It's an invitation.

A chance to fill that space with your true self.

So don't fear the nights you sleep alone.

Don't fear the days when no one asks how you are.

Don't fear...

This loneliness is a road—

And if you walk it,

you'll find yourself at the end.

And once you find yourself,

no one,

and nothing,

can take that peace away from you.

Chapter Twelve: Hope – A Light in the Darkness

Sometimes life grows so dark that not even the smallest glimmer of light can be seen.

No signs. No voices. No hand to hold.

Only the darkness—and your exhaustion.

In those moments,

hope feels like a distant myth.

You ask:

"Hope? For what? When nothing ever changes? When the harder I try, the more I break?"

But hope isn't something big.

Hope is just one breath…

The breath you take when you think you can't go on—

But still, you breathe.

Hope is waking up with tears,

but still getting out of bed.

It's when your heart still beats for a future,

even in the middle of despair.

It's when a single flower on a cracked sidewalk warms your chest.

Hope isn't a scream.

Sometimes, it's just a whisper.

A voice only you can hear,

saying: "Try one more time… just one more."

People live on hope.

Not on memories.

Not on promises.

You keep going because something inside you still believes.

And don't forget—

Hope doesn't come from someone else's hands.

You have to find it yourself.

In your pain.

In your quiet.

In that one moment where everything seems lost

that's when hope is born.

Even if it's just a flicker,

that flicker is enough to see the path again.

And you—

no matter how tired you are,

no matter how broken—

You deserve that flicker.

Because you're still alive.

And as long as you breathe,

you still can.

There is still time.

Chapter Thirteen: Healing – The Art of Becoming Whole Again

Healing doesn't come all at once.

It doesn't shout, it doesn't arrive with a clear sign.

It's quiet. Subtle.

Like the way the sky slowly lightens before dawn.

Some days you'll feel like you're moving forward—

smiling, breathing, maybe even laughing.

And some days…

You'll fall back into the ache,

into the old thoughts, the old fears.

And that's okay.

Because healing is not a straight line.

It's a messy, beautiful, winding road.

You will have to visit the same pain more than once.

Not because you failed,

but because you're learning to face it—layer by layer.

Healing means

letting the wound breathe.

It means saying,

"Yes, this hurt me. And yes, I'm still here."

It means being patient with yourself.

Not rushing your heart to be "okay."

Not forcing your smile to return too soon.

You're allowed to feel tired.

You're allowed to take breaks.

You're allowed to rest inside the silence.

And remember—

Healing does not mean the pain never existed.

It means it no longer controls you.

It means you can look at the scar,

and instead of breaking,

you nod softly and say:

"This is a part of me. But it's not all of me."

Every time you choose to be gentle with yourself,

every time you cry and still choose to keep going,

every time you forgive yourself a little more—

You are healing.

Slowly, steadily,

you are becoming whole again.

Not who you were before the pain—

But someone wiser. Softer. Stronger.

You are not broken beyond repair.

You are becoming.

Chapter Fourteen: Love – An Embrace Beyond Words

Love isn't always what you see in movies.

It doesn't always come with flowers, with music,

or with long, poetic embraces.

Sometimes… It's quiet.

Simple.

And it just is.

Real love is not rescue.

No one is coming to erase all your pain.

No one is meant to "complete" you.

You are not half.

You are already more whole than you realize.

Love, sometimes, is just listening.

It's someone who hears you without needing to fix you.

Someone who stays without needing constant words.

Someone who sees your silence and says,

"I'm here. Still."

Love isn't in the one who says, "I will complete you,"

But in the one who says,

"I see you—just as you are—and I'm still here."

We often mistake love—

confusing it with need, with fear, with loneliness.

But true love breathes in open spaces.

In the freedom to be fully yourself,

without editing, without shrinking,

without proving your worth.

Love is safety.

Not unstable passion.

Not games.

But the kind of safety that lets you ask:

"If one day I'm afraid… will you still love me?

If my old wounds return… will you stay?"

And love replies:

"Yes. Because I chose you, not your perfection."

And more than anything…

Love must begin within.

You must see yourself, deeply.

Hold yourself with compassion.

So that any love from outside

is only a reflection of the love already blooming inside you.

You deserve a love that steadies you—

not one that becomes a weight.

You deserve a love that helps you grow—

not one that silences your light.

And until that love arrives—

wait.

Or better yet, be it.

And let love, quiet and steady,

find its way to you

when you least expect it…

and most deserve it.

Chapter Fifteen: Release – A Place to Breathe

Release doesn't always mean cutting ties.

Sometimes, it's just a quiet yes—

to yourself.

To the part of you that no longer wants to stay chained,

to the part that's tired of fighting battles that were never yours to begin with.

Release isn't about leaving a relationship,

or erasing a memory,

or pretending someone never mattered.

It's about accepting that some things will remain unfinished—

And that their incompletion

is not your failure.

You have the right to walk away from what hurts you,

even if you once called it love.

Even if others don't understand,

judge you,

or say, "You're just too sensitive."

Release is self-respect.

It's saying:

"I deserve peace.

I deserve a smile that comes from within,

not one I wear to make others comfortable."

Sometimes, you have to let something old fall apart,

so there's room for something new to breathe—

for light to enter.

You're not meant to be everyone's hero.

You're not meant to carry the weight forever.

Sometimes, release means sitting down,

letting the tears come,

and whispering:

"I can't hold this anymore."

And there, within the softness of surrender—

In the quiet between the sobs,

you'll find a space

just wide enough

to breathe.

Release is not a point in time—

It's a path.

A path of recognition, forgiveness, and letting go.

And you, right now, are walking it…

toward peace.

Chapter Sixteen: Forgiveness – A Gentle Touch on Silent Wounds

Forgiveness is not forgetting.

Not erasing.

Not simply moving on from what hurt you.

Forgiveness is a choice—

not because they deserve it,

but because you do.

You deserve peace.

Sometimes we stay stuck in the past,

not because we love it,

but because we haven't yet learned

how to forgive ourselves

for the pain we allowed in.

Forgiveness is saying:

"Yes, it hurt.

But I don't want this pain to greet me every morning anymore."

Sometimes, the one who needs your forgiveness the most

is you.

For staying too long.

For silencing your inner voice.

For looking away from truths

because facing them felt too heavy.

You are human.

And humans make mistakes.

But the real ache isn't in the mistake itself—

It's in the refusal

to hold ourselves with tenderness.

Forgiveness is a soft touch on your wounds.

Not to erase them,

but so you no longer have to live

in their shadow.

You have the right to be free—

from the past,

from the voice inside that whispers,

"You should have known better."

No.

You knew exactly what you could know at the time.

And that was enough.

Begin today

with a little more kindness toward yourself.

Place your hand on your heart and say:

"I'm still here, with all my scars—

And I still deserve peace."

And that

is the beginning of forgiveness…

Chapter Seventeen: Hope – A Light That Doesn't Go Out

Hope isn't always loud.

Sometimes, it's just a quiet breath

in the middle of a silent cry.

Sometimes, it's simply standing—

not moving, not fighting—just standing.

Hope doesn't shout.

It doesn't make grand promises.

Hope lives in the eyes of someone

who, despite all the heartbreak,

still greets the morning.

You don't have to be endlessly positive.

You don't have to pretend you're okay.

Hope isn't born from pretending.

It comes from honesty—

from that soft whisper that says:

"I'm tired… but I haven't given up."

Sometimes hope

is just surviving the night

without hating yourself.

It's letting yourself miss something,

letting the tears fall,

but still… still thinking,

maybe tomorrow.

Hope belongs to the brave—

not the fearless,

but the ones who live with fear

and still leave space

for light to enter.

If today is heavy,

if giving up feels easier—

That's okay.

But don't forget:

there's something inside you

that's still holding on.

Hold that part.

Call it by its name:

Hope.

And if you can't find any light—

then be the candle,

trembling in the dark,

but refusing to go out.

Chapter Eighteen: Acceptance – An Embrace for All of You

Acceptance means seeing yourself as you are—

not as others expect you to be.

Not as social media tells you to look or live.

Just… you.

With all your flaws, fears, wounds,

and even the parts you still don't know how to love.

Acceptance isn't giving up.

It isn't letting go.

It's honesty—

The kind that softly says:

"This is me,

and that's enough."

We're taught to always be better,

but rarely do we learn

how to love who we are right now.

Acceptance is kindness toward yourself

on days you did nothing but survive—

And that alone was a victory.

It's learning to love your voice,

your body, your past,

and not being afraid of mirrors

that show the truth without filters.

Acceptance means you stop waiting

for someone else to say,

"You are enough."

And instead,

you say it to yourself.

Out loud.

And believe it.

You don't need to be perfect

to be worthy of love.

You only need to be—

to stay,

and slowly learn that being

is already beautiful.

Chapter Nineteen: A New Beginning – When You Think It's All Over

Sometimes, you think it's all over.

That there's no chance to begin again.

That which was meant to happen has already happened,

and now you just have to live with what's left.

But the truth is,

in every ending,

in every moment that feels like something has broken,

there's always a chance for a new beginning.

Not to forget what's happened,

but to remember that

you're still here,

and you can choose what to make of this moment.

A new beginning isn't about going back.

It's a step forward—

a choice to move toward the light

when everything around you seems dark.

You may see your mistakes,

your wounds,

but none of those define you.

You are strong enough to rebuild—

not from scratch,

but from exactly where you stand.

A new beginning isn't about running away.

It's about standing firm in the face of what is,

and telling yourself:

"Yes, I may be broken,

but I can still fly."

Every day is a new beginning.

Every moment, every small decision,

is an opportunity to create something new.

And remember:

You are never too late to start over.

You can always create a better tomorrow.

Chapter Twenty: Peace – Making Peace with Life

In the end, life isn't meant to be perfect.

Things won't always go as planned,

people won't always stay,

and wounds won't always heal without pain.

But you can make peace with life—

not because it's flawless,

but because it's real.

Peace lives in the acceptance of imperfection.

In breathing between the ache and the ease.

In realizing that life is a blend of

comings and goings,

tears and laughter,

and you, right in the middle of it all,

can still be okay.

Making peace with life means putting down the fight.

Not out of defeat,

but out of wisdom.

It means letting go of the need to control everything,

and allowing the world to be as it is—

And you,

as you are.

Sometimes there is nothing to fix.

There is only something to feel—

and let it pass through you,

like wind through trees.

You find peace

when you stop seeing yourself as a project to repair,

and start seeing yourself as a living, growing being—

full of lines, pauses, and space.

Life won't always be easy,

But you can be gentle with it.

And that gentleness,

slowly,

brings you home to yourself.

Chapter Twenty-One: Silence – Where Everything Begins

Silence isn't always empty.

Sometimes, it's fuller than any word.

Silence is the space between two heartbeats,

between two breaths,

between two choices.

In a world that shouts,

that constantly demands your voice, your action,

silence is a form of courage.

Silence means sitting beside yourself

with no need to speak,

no urge to judge,

and simply… being.

It's in the quiet where your truth begins to echo.

Where your heart starts to speak—

softly, without noise,

and more honestly than any scream.

Silence says:

"Look. You are here. You are alive. You are enough."

And that voice,

though gentle,

can shift your entire inner world.

You don't always need answers.

You don't always need direction.

Sometimes,

you just need to stay quiet

and let the path reveal itself to you.

Silence is not the end—

It's the beginning.

A beginning where you finally hear yourself

in a world full of noise,

but only you can recognize your true voice.

Chapter Twenty-Two: Trust – Letting Yourself Fall Into Life's Path

Trust means not knowing everything

and still taking the next step.

It's finding your way

not with a perfect map,

but with your heart.

Trust is believing

that even when nothing goes as planned,

something is still unfolding—

Something you might not see yet,

but one day, you will understand.

We've been taught to control,

to figure everything out, to predict and plan,

but life arrives with its own stories—

unexpected,

and because of that, alive.

To trust is to release yourself

into the current of life,

not knowing where you'll end up,

but believing that you will arrive.

Sometimes, you don't need all the answers.

You only need to say:

"I don't know… but I believe."

And that one sentence

can lighten the weight of all your questions.

Trust means that if you get lost,

if you fall,

if the road goes dark…

you still know the path

will somehow reveal itself.

Trust feels like flying through fog—

You can't see what's ahead,

but you spread your wings

and go.

Chapter Twenty-Three: Hope – A Light That Rises From Within

Hope isn't always loud.

Sometimes it has no sound,

just a quiet glow

that gently shines through the dark.

Hope means you still believe

that something good is on its way—

not because everything is easy,

but because you

are no longer the person you used to be.

Sometimes, hope is simply standing up again.

Even when no one sees you.

Even when a voice inside whispers, "What's the point?"

You still answer, softly:

"Maybe not today,

but someday…"

Hope isn't about clinging to the future—

It's about trusting the strength within you

that keeps choosing life

in this very moment.

Hope isn't always cheerful.

Sometimes it comes with tears, with weariness, with silence.

And yet, it stays,

and somehow, it carries you forward.

Hope means knowing:

Yes, there is darkness,

but there's also a light within you

that—even if it flickers—

It is enough to guide the way.

And that light,

it doesn't come from somewhere far—

It comes from you.

Chapter Twenty-Four: Acceptance – An Embrace for the Present Moment

Acceptance means laying down your weapons.

Not in defeat,

but in the realization

that the moment you're standing in

is not your enemy.

Acceptance is saying to life:

"Be, just as you are."

And saying to yourself:

"I will be, just as I am."

We're used to clinging to the past,

or fearing the future.

But the only place where life truly lives

is here, in this moment.

And this moment—

With all its flaws and gaps—

deserves to be seen.

Acceptance is loving yourself

even when things are still messy.

It's telling your heart:

"You don't have to be perfect,

you just have to be true."

Acceptance is being kind to what is—

to the mistakes, the wounds, the feelings you don't yet understand.

It's not about giving up on growth,

but about giving up the war against yourself.

In acceptance, there is a peace

that nothing else can offer.

A peace that doesn't say, "Everything is great,"

but gently says,

"You, as you are, are enough."

Chapter Twenty-Five: A New Beginning – When the Heart Opens Again

Sometimes, everything doesn't need to be rebuilt.

You just need your heart…

to open once more.

Maybe not with force or excitement,

but gently—

like a bud sensing the return of spring.

New beginnings aren't always loud.

Sometimes, they're just a deep breath

after days of silence and held-back tears.

Sometimes, they sound like:

"I'm still here… and I still want to try."

Even a heart that has broken many times

can open again.

Not because it has forgotten,

but because it has learned—

Breaking is not the end.

A new beginning means giving yourself permission

to trust again,

to laugh again,

to touch life again

without shame for the wounds you carry.

It means knowing:

Nothing is ever truly lost.

As long as you breathe,

there is still space for becoming, for change, for love.

And this is the most beautiful kind of beginning—

When, from the depth of darkness,

not through force, not in a rush,

but with softness and honesty,

you whisper to yourself once more:

"Come back… There is still time."

Chapter Twenty-Six: Solitude – Where Your Voice Becomes Clearer

Solitude isn't always painful.

Sometimes, it's an invitation.

A quiet space

where your true voice can finally be heard.

We fear being alone,

because we think it means something is missing—

That being alone is a failure.

But solitude can be a sign of growth,

a sign that you're no longer willing

to fill your heart

with just anything.

Solitude, when met with awareness,

becomes sacred.

Not emptiness, but space.

Not distance, but closeness to yourself.

In your aloneness, you can breathe.

You can write, read, think,

and most of all—

You can listen to what you truly want.

Those who have made peace with their solitude

are powerful—

not dangerous to others,

but to anything that tried to keep them dependent.

Because once you've lived with yourself,

you know:

being with another should be a choice,

not a need.

Not an escape.

And that's when connection becomes meaningful—

not when you run from being alone,

but when, from the wholeness of your being,

you choose to walk toward someone.

Chapter Twenty-Seven: Letting Go – When You Allow What Must, to Leave

Letting go doesn't always come with a scream.

Sometimes, it arrives with a sigh,

a bittersweet smile,

or just one quiet sentence:

"That's enough…"

We are taught to hold on—

to people, to memories,

to dreams that no longer breathe.

Because we think if we let go,

we'll lose a part of ourselves.

But sometimes, it's the opposite:

When you release,

you return to yourself.

Letting go is the moment you realize

you cannot save everything.

Not every relationship,

not every version of your past,

not even the version of you

that no longer feels real.

Letting go takes courage—

not to fight,

but to stop holding on.

To walk away,

without bitterness.

To set something down,

without needing to forget.

Letting go means holding yourself

in the quiet afterward,

and whispering:

"I'm still here.

Lighter,

but more whole."

And in that lightness,

a space opens—

for the things waiting to find you.

For what you deserve,

not just what you've been used to.

Chapter Twenty-Eight: Unfinished – The Beauty of What Isn't Complete

Not everything is meant to be whole.

Not everything needs a clean ending,

or a perfect conclusion.

Sometimes, being unfinished…

It is the most honest way to exist.

We're used to closure—

to periods, to answers, to neat resolutions.

But life is more like an ellipsis…

like sentences that trail off,

and feelings that never get fully explained.

There is beauty in the unfinished.

Because it leaves room—

for wonder, for growth,

for the quiet knowing

that something is still left to be felt,

to be lived, to be discovered.

We ourselves are unfinished.

And maybe that's what keeps us alive.

If you ever feel like you have to figure it all out,

to tie up every thread,

to close every door—

Remember this:

Unfinished doesn't mean broken.

It means brave.

It means you're living with the unknown,

and still choosing to love, to forgive, to breathe.

Some wounds never fully close.

Some people never return.

Some questions go unanswered.

But even with all of that—

You can keep going.

You can say:

"I am not complete.

But I still dream, I still feel,

and that is more than enough."

Chapter Twenty-Nine: Making Peace with Yourself – Befriending the One You See in the Mirror

Making peace with yourself is a long journey.

Not a fleeting moment,

but sometimes it takes a lifetime to realize

that the person you see in the mirror,

just as they are,

is already whole.

We've always searched outside ourselves

for someone to see us, understand us, love us.

But in the end, it is we who must

first learn to love ourselves.

Making peace with yourself means accepting

that no one is perfect.

Not you, not the person you want to become.

And not the reflection you see.

But with all those flaws and mistakes,

you are everything you need to be.

When you make peace with yourself,

you no longer fear the inner criticisms.

In fact, you laugh at them

because you know these voices

are just part of the story.

And you will never become the whole story.

Your story is always in the making.

Making peace with yourself means finding peace

in the face of inadequacies,

seeing your struggles not as weakness,

but as a path to growth and deeper understanding.

And most importantly,

making peace with yourself means accepting

that you are worthy of all the love you seek—

not the love that is validated from the outside,

but the unconditional love from within.

When you make peace with yourself,

everything changes.

The outside world may stay the same,

but your inner world becomes a symphony of new colors and sounds.

And in this fresh world,

anything is possible.

Chapter Thirty: Receiving Love from Within – Remembering That You Must First Love Yourself

We've always sought love from the outside.

In the gaze of others, in their approval,

in their words and embraces.

But the truth is:

Real love comes from within.

This love isn't from the person who sees you as whole,

but from your acceptance of yourself.

It's learning to love yourself without judgment,

with all your flaws, with all your failures,

and even with all the emotions you feel in the moment.

Love from within means

learning to be kind to yourself,

even when you feel inadequate.

It means forgiving yourself,

not just for mistakes,

but for all the hard moments you've been through.

Love from within is a journey.

Not a fixed destination, but a path that takes you

to a deeper understanding of yourself.

This journey may take time,

but with every step, every moment, you see yourself more clearly,

it reminds you:

You are worthy of a love

that begins from within.

This love doesn't seek anything,

but is love itself—

And once you find this love inside you,

external loves are no longer needs,

but additions to what you've already discovered within.

Chapter Thirty-One: Small Miracles – Recognizing the Magic of Every Day

Life doesn't exist in the big moments.

In truth, all of its beauty lies in the small moments—

In the brief glance you share with someone,

in the silent smile,

in that deep breath you take after a long day.

We search for grand magic,

while all the magic is in the small things.

In the cup of coffee you drink with care,

in the sound of rain falling on the window,

in the beam of sunlight filtering through the trees.

Small moments are miraculous

because they're always with us,

and we often don't notice them.

They're the moments that, as time passes,

live on unnoticed.

If we pay a little more attention,

we'll see that in these ordinary moments,

there is something extraordinary—

In every step, in every breath,

in every meeting, in every silence.

These moments remind us that

life, as it is, is beautiful.

It doesn't need to be perfect,

because the wonder is in the imperfection.

In the small details that make life come alive.

When we learn to enjoy these small moments,

life begins to smile at us in a new way.

And then we realize that each day,

has its own magic.

Chapter Thirty-Two: Remembering the Magic of Today – Living in the Present Moment

We spend so much time chasing tomorrow,

believing that happiness is always ahead of us,

somewhere in the future.

But the truth is,

the magic has always been right here, right now.

Today is its own kind of miracle.

It's a moment to be alive,

to breathe, to feel, to exist.

We don't always notice the magic of today—

the simple things, the small joys,

the way the sun kisses your skin,

the laughter of a friend,

the warmth of a hug.

Every day is filled with a kind of quiet magic,

waiting to be seen, felt, and appreciated.

But we have to be present to experience it.

We have to stop running toward an imagined future

and start living in the here and now.

When we focus on today,

we realize that it's enough.

We don't need to have it all figured out,

we don't need to wait for a perfect tomorrow.

Today, there's already a universe of beauty,

a world of possibilities.

So, today, pause.

Look around.

Feel the world beneath your feet,

the air in your lungs,

the rhythm of your heartbeat.

This is the magic of now.

Chapter Thirty-Three: The Embrace of Life – Accepting What We Have

Life doesn't always unfold the way we want it to.

Sometimes, in the twists and turns of the journey,

we find ourselves having to settle for something different from what we imagined.

But perhaps, within these incomplete and imperfect things,

lies the secret to beauty.

The embrace of life shows us that

accepting what we have doesn't mean giving up.

Rather, it means understanding that

this very moment, this very situation,

is all we need to grow and experience.

We are always searching for something more, better, and more complete.

But the truth is that

what we have right now, just as it is,

is enough.

Life is found in those moments where we realize who we are,

not in the moments we wish to reach.

Acceptance of life doesn't mean being content with circumstances.

It means seeing the beauty in everything we have,

in everything we're currently experiencing,

and in ourselves, just as we are.

The embrace of life teaches us that

not only should we accept ourselves,

but we should also embrace the world outside just as it is.

For everything in our lives

is part of us and part of our journey.

In this embrace, nothing is meaningless.

Every failure, every victory,

every moment of joy and sorrow,

all connect and lead us toward greater self-awareness and acceptance.

So today, say to life:

"I accept you. Just as you are, just as I am.

Your embrace will always be open to me."

Chapter Thirty-Four: Remembering the Power of Difficult Moments

We are always afraid of the hard moments.

Of pain, of failure, of sorrow.

But the truth is that

these difficult moments are the ones that shape us.

Hard moments teach us

that there is light hidden within the darkness.

They show us that

we should cherish the good days even more

and learn lessons from the pain that can't be found in any book.

It's these hard moments that bring us closer to our true selves.

They tell us that

we have the strength to overcome any challenge,

that within ourselves, we have the power to grow and change.

In the midst of difficult moments,

you might feel like everything is over.

But it's exactly in these moments

that you are growing and transforming into a stronger version of yourself.

Pain is not always the enemy.

Sometimes, it's our greatest teacher.

And when we come out the other side,

we realize that these struggles, in a beautiful way,

have turned us into better versions of ourselves.

So when you face difficult moments,

remember that each moment

is an opportunity for learning and growth.

And tell yourself:

"This is part of the journey. I am capable of getting through it."

Chapter Thirty-Five: The Power of Simply Being

We are always striving to be more.

More successful, more joyful, more perfect.

But the truth is that

sometimes, simplicity is the most powerful thing.

Being in the moment, without any extra effort,

without worrying about the future or regretting the past,

this is the simplest and yet most profound way of living.

In this simplicity lies the truth of our existence.

When we let go of all the stress and pressures

and simply allow ourselves to be,

that's when we can discover the magic of life.

We only need to breathe, feel,

and enjoy every moment we have.

The power lies in not needing to prove anything.

We only need to be ourselves,

and from that being, we touch the whole world.

In every breath we take,

in every step we make,

in every glance and smile we share,

there is hidden strength.

This power is the power of acceptance.

Acceptance of ourselves and of what we have right now.

Acceptance of this moment, this situation, this self.

And in this acceptance, growth and transformation happen.

So in this noisy, pressurized world,

remember that simply being

can be the greatest power.

Right now, just be.

And let the power of simplicity flow through you.

Chapter Thirty-Six: The Beauty in Incompletion – Not Perfect, but Alive

The world has taught us that being perfect is the ultimate goal.

That if there's failure, lack, scars, or doubt—

Then somehow, we're not "enough."

But the truth of life is the exact opposite.

Real beauty lives in the incomplete.

In the cracks where light gets in,

in the stories that are still unfolding,

in the people who are still learning, growing, becoming.

To be unfinished is to be alive.

It means there is still room to move,

to explore, to experience, to learn.

If everything were perfect and done,

what would life even mean?

Incompletion means we are still becoming.

And that becoming—

that journey—

It is a gift in itself.

We are on the path, not at the destination.

And the path, with all its bumps and bends,

is far more beautiful than any flawless picture.

So give yourself permission to be incomplete.

Let some days be about simply being.

Not being better, not being more—

just being.

And when you begin to see that your imperfections are part of your beauty,

a deep peace begins to grow inside you.

Because you realize:

you don't have to fix everything,

you don't have to be like anyone else.

You, just as you are—unfinished,

are endlessly beautiful and real.

Chapter Thirty-Seven: Making Peace with the Past

We all carry stories.

Some we whisper.

Some we bury so deep we forget they ever happened—until something brings them back.

The past has a way of lingering,

of echoing through our present moments,

shaping the way we love, trust, fear, and hope.

But here's the truth:

You are not what happened to you.

You are what you choose to become,

even with the weight of your yesterdays on your shoulders.

Making peace with the past doesn't mean forgetting.

It means forgiving yourself for not knowing better.

It means releasing the need to rewrite what has already been written.

It means finally exhaling the pain

you've been holding in your chest for far too long.

There's power in looking back with gentle eyes.

Not to judge,

but to understand.

To see the scared version of yourself and say,

"I get it. You did what you could with what you had."

Healing isn't linear.

Some days you'll feel like you've let go.

Other days, the old ache returns,

familiar and sharp.

But that, too, is part of the process.

Peace doesn't always come loudly.

Sometimes, it arrives quietly,

in a moment where you no longer feel the need to explain,

to fight,

or to run.

It comes when you realize that the past cannot hurt you in the same way anymore—

because you've grown beyond it.

You've given yourself permission to move forward.

So today, let the past be a place of reference, not residence.

Take what you've learned.

Honor what you've survived.

And walk on—lighter, freer, whole.

Chapter Thirty-Eight: Trusting the Unknown Future

As humans, we crave certainty.

We want to know what's coming, control it, and predict it.

And when the future becomes uncertain,

our hearts tremble,

as if we've been left defenseless in a storm of "what ifs."

But the truth is:

Life always happens in the unknown.

In the places with no map,

where your heart still beats and says,

"Keep going."

Trusting the future means trusting yourself,

even when you don't know what's ahead.

It means saying,

"I don't know what's coming,

but I know I'll make it through."

Sometimes you have to let go of what no longer serves you,

to make space for what hasn't arrived yet—

But it is on its way.

Trust is understanding a simple, powerful truth:

The universe is not against you.

Some things don't break you—

They wake you up.

And when you stop clinging to certainty,

and offer your hand to life,

you slowly begin to learn

that surrender isn't weakness—

It's courage.

So if the future feels unclear,

if you don't know what your next step is—

That's okay.

You don't have to know it all.

You just have to believe that with every step,

the path will reveal itself.

You were made for this.

Even in the dark, there is light guiding you forward—

And that light lives within you.

Chapter Thirty-Nine: The Art of Letting Go

Letting go is not giving up.

It's not weakness.

It's not failure.

It's a quiet decision to stop carrying what is too heavy to hold.

What no longer helps you grow.

There are things we cling to—

old wounds, past lovers, lost chances,

versions of ourselves we've outgrown.

We hold on out of habit, out of fear, out of the illusion that without them, we won't know who we are.

But there comes a moment—

gentle, or sudden—

When your soul whispers,

"It's time."

Time to release the weight,

to open your hands,

to breathe again.

Letting go is a practice,

not a one-time act.

It's waking up each day and choosing not to reopen old stories.

It's choosing presence over pain,

peace over pride.

You don't have to forget what happened.

You don't have to pretend it didn't matter.

But you can choose to no longer let it define you.

Sometimes we don't heal by holding on.

We heal by loosening our grip.

And when you finally let go—

of expectations, of control, of what could've been—

You create space.

Space for clarity.

Space for love.

Space for life to surprise you again.

So let it go.

Not because it wasn't real,

but because you are—

And you deserve to move forward free.

Chapter Forty: Returning to Your True Self

In all the roles you've played,

in all the ways you've changed to be accepted,

in all the versions of yourself you've created to survive—

One part of you has always remained:

your true self.

Not the one who always had it together,

not the perfect one,

but the one who was real.

With doubts, with feelings, with dreams, with scars.

Returning to yourself

isn't about going backward.

It's about coming home—

to a place where no approval is needed,

where your own voice is finally heard again,

and where who you are is enough.

Sometimes, this return comes after getting lost.

After chasing paths that never felt like yours.

After exhausting yourself trying to please, impress, or be loved.

And then, quietly, something inside you says:

"You're tired… It's time to come back."

So you return—

not to the person you were,

but to the truth you've always carried.

You learn that you don't need to be someone else.

You don't need to be better than others.

You learn that honesty is power,

and that kindness toward yourself is where real change begins.

Returning to your true self means looking in the mirror and saying,

"This is me—and this is enough."

You don't need to become someone new.

You just need to clear away the dust

so the real you can rise again.

Home has always been here—

Within you.

And now that you've returned,

breathe.

Be still.

And welcome yourself back.

Chapter Forty-One: The Power of Silence

In a world that is constantly loud—

where every moment is filled with noise,

opinions, judgments, expectations—

Silence becomes a sanctuary.

It is not emptiness.

It is space.

It is the stillness where we can hear ourselves think,

feel our hearts beat,

and find the truth that often gets drowned out by the world.

Silence doesn't need words to speak.

It holds more wisdom than a thousand conversations.

It is in the quiet moments that we can connect with the deepest parts of ourselves,

the parts that have been waiting for us to listen.

Sometimes, silence is the answer.

Not everything needs to be said.

Not every question needs to be answered right away.

In the stillness, we allow clarity to come, not forced,

but gently, like a breeze on a quiet morning.

There is power in pausing—

In giving yourself permission to be still.

It's in these moments that you reconnect with what truly matters.

It's when you step back from the noise of life and allow your inner voice to be heard.

We are often afraid of silence.

Afraid of the thoughts that might surface,

the feelings we may have to confront,

the discomfort of simply being.

But silence is not the enemy.

It is the bridge to peace.

The place where healing happens.

The space where our true selves can finally be.

So, embrace silence.

Sit in it, breathe in it,

and let it reveal what words never could.

In the quiet, you will find everything you need—

not in the answers,

but in the questions that remain.

Chapter Forty-Two: Embracing Life in the Present Moment

All you need in this moment is right here.

Not in the past, not in the future,

but in this very now.

The moment you are standing in,

the moment you are breathing in,

the moment where nothing else matters but here and now.

Life is always moving—

And we often give all our attention to the past,

or worry about a future that hasn't yet arrived.

But in the process, the present moment slips away.

The moment that could be your source of peace, joy, and connection with yourself.

The embrace of life is in this moment.

In the place where you can, for a second,

put aside all your efforts, all your worries, and all the outside pressures

and just be.

Just feel, just see,

just breathe.

If you can let go in this moment,

if you can embrace this moment,

you will see that everything changes.

Life will show itself to you—

not in the face of stress and pressure,

but in the face of calm, in the face of acceptance.

Every moment is an opportunity to start anew,

to release everything that shouldn't be.

And to remember this simple truth:

You are enough, just as you are.

In the embrace of the present moment, there's nothing to prove.

Nothing to rush toward.

Only here and now, where you must be present.

So, embrace this moment.

Now, not tomorrow.

Right now.

And see how life, in all its simplicity,

will respond to you in the very moment you give it your full attention.

Chapter Forty-Three: The Power of Accepting Failure

Failure isn't the end of the road.

It isn't a mark of who you are,

or a reflection of your worth.

Failure is simply a step along the journey—

a teacher, a reminder that you are human,

and that growth often comes in the form of setbacks.

When we fail, we are often quick to judge ourselves.

We label ourselves as not good enough,

or as unworthy of success.

But the truth is, failure doesn't define you.

What defines you is how you rise from it.

What defines you is your ability to keep moving forward,

to learn, to adapt, and to try again.

In the moments of failure, we are given the chance to learn who we truly are—

not through success,

but through our resilience, our perseverance, and our capacity to embrace imperfection.

Failure is not something to fear.

It is not something to avoid.

It is an opportunity to grow stronger,

to become more compassionate with yourself,

and to understand that every misstep is just a part of the greater journey.

So let go of the shame you carry for failing.

Let go of the fear that tells you you're not enough.

And instead, embrace failure as part of your story.

Because in the end, it's not about how many times you fall,

but about how many times you get back up.

Failure is a gift—

a stepping stone on the path to becoming the best version of yourself.

So accept it, learn from it,

and keep moving forward.

Chapter Forty-Four: Embracing Change

Change is the only constant in life.

Though we may feel resistance to every change, the truth is that change is an opportunity for growth and transformation.

Not a threat, not something to run from, but a gateway to new experiences.

We are naturally drawn to stability and security.

We want life to unfold exactly as we wish,

for each day to be like the one before.

But life doesn't stand still, and time is always moving forward.

Embracing change means embracing the flow of life.

It means allowing life to reshape itself,

without constantly trying to control it.

It means understanding that every change, whether big or small,

is ultimately leading us to where we need to be.

Sometimes, changes can be frightening.

Sometimes, we might feel like we're losing something,

or heading toward something we don't want.

But we must learn that within change, there are always new possibilities.

Change can be an opportunity to find our true selves,

to discover strengths we didn't know we had,

to face parts of ourselves we've long ignored.

Change, with all its challenges, is sometimes the only way for us to become the best version of ourselves.

So instead of fighting change,

let's learn to embrace it.

Let's understand that change is part of the process of life,

and that every change is a step toward something better.

When we embrace change,

we stand stronger in the face of life's storms.

When we accept that change is always happening,

life becomes an exciting journey

where nothing is set in stone,

but everything is possible.

Chapter Forty-Five: Empowering Yourself

There is a quiet strength within you—

one that doesn't shout or demand attention,

but simply exists, steady and constant.

It's the part of you that knows how to keep going

even when everything feels heavy.

It's the voice that whispers, "You can,"

even when the world seems to say, "You can't."

Empowering yourself doesn't always look like bold action.

Sometimes, it looks like getting out of bed when your heart feels tired.

Sometimes, it's saying no.

Sometimes, it's choosing rest instead of pushing through.

Sometimes, it's asking for help without shame.

To empower yourself is to trust yourself.

To believe that your voice matters,

that your needs are valid,

and that your boundaries are sacred.

It means taking ownership of your story,

even the parts that hurt.

It means recognizing that healing isn't linear,

and growth doesn't always feel graceful—

But both are still powerful.

True empowerment comes from within.

Not from titles, or approval, or applause—

But from the quiet moments when you decide

that you are worthy of love,

worthy of peace,

worthy of choosing yourself.

So give yourself permission—

to speak, to rest, to change, to begin again.

You don't need to be perfect to be powerful.

You only need to be real.

And you already are.

Chapter Forty-Six: Letting Go of Control

Sometimes you try so hard to hold everything together,

to predict every outcome,

to avoid every risk,

that you forget—

Life was never meant to be controlled in the first place.

Letting go isn't weakness.

It's trust.

Trust in yourself,

trust in time,

trust in a path you may not fully see yet,

but deep down, you know it is unfolding for you.

We often believe that control will keep us safe.

But true safety comes from surrender.

From taking a deep breath and saying:

"I don't know what's next, but I'll let it come."

Over-controlling disconnects you from the present.

It fills your mind with fear,

and your heart with pressure.

But when you release the grip,

when you stop swimming against the current,

peace starts to return.

You don't have to know everything.

You don't have to fix it all,

or hold everyone together.

Sometimes, the bravest thing you can do

is to breathe, take a step,

and trust the flow.

Letting go is not giving up—

It's choosing to believe that some things

are best left to time and life itself.

So let what needs to fall away, fall.

Let what needs to arrive, arrive.

And let yourself find calm

in the quiet space that opens

when you finally loosen your grip.

Chapter Forty-Seven: Embracing Solitude

There's a kind of peace that only comes

when the world goes quiet.

When it's just you—

no noise, no distractions,

just the soft rhythm of your own breath

and the thoughts you've long tried to outrun.

Solitude isn't loneliness.

It's presence.

It's choosing to sit with yourself

without needing to be filled, fixed, or entertained.

In solitude, you start to remember things.

The sound of your own heartbeat.

The feel of silence resting gently on your skin.

The parts of you that get drowned out in the chaos.

Being alone can be uncomfortable at first.

It brings you face-to-face with your fears,

your doubts, your longings.

But it also brings clarity.

It teaches you to be your own anchor,

your own comfort, your own home.

Solitude is where you come back to yourself.

It's where you unlearn the noise of the world

and relearn the language of your soul.

You don't have to be afraid of being alone.

Because in that stillness,

you'll find the pieces of you that were never truly lost—

just waiting to be heard.

So take the time.

Sit with yourself.

Let silence be your teacher.

And trust that in the space where no one else is speaking,

your own voice will finally rise.

Chapter Forty-Eight: Listening to Your Inner Voice

There is a voice inside you—

quiet, gentle,

but full of truth.

It doesn't scream.

It doesn't beg for attention.

It whispers.

Softly, patiently,

waiting for the moment when you're finally still enough to hear it.

In a world filled with noise—

opinions, expectations, comparisons—

it's easy to lose touch with that voice.

To forget that the answers you're chasing

might already be living inside you.

Your inner voice knows.

It knows what feels right and what doesn't.

It knows what you need,

even when your mind is clouded with confusion.

Listening to that voice takes courage.

Because sometimes, it will guide you down paths that feel uncertain.

Sometimes, it will ask you to let go, to say no,

to walk away from things that look "right" but feel wrong.

But trust it.

That voice is your compass.

It's your truest self,

the part of you untouched by fear or pressure.

You don't need to have all the answers right now.

You just need to be quiet enough

to hear your heart when it speaks.

So make space.

Turn down the noise.

Sit in the stillness.

And when that quiet voice rises from within,

listen.

Because it's always been speaking.

And it always leads you home.

Chapter Forty-Nine: The Beauty of Beginning Again

There is something quietly powerful

about starting over.

About saying:

"I thought I knew the way… but maybe it's time for a new one."

We often think beginning again means we failed.

That we lost something.

But the truth is—

Beginning again means we're still growing.

Still learning.

Still brave enough to try.

There's beauty in starting from where you are,

with what you have,

even if all you have is a tired heart

and a small spark of hope.

Sometimes the reset is not loud.

It's not some big event.

It's a quiet moment of choosing differently.

Choosing to breathe,

to let go,

to believe again.

Each sunrise is an invitation:

to forgive yourself,

to rewrite the story,

to walk into the unknown, not with fear,

but with softness in your heart.

You are not starting from scratch.

You are starting from experience.

From strength.

From lessons you've earned.

And no matter how many times you begin again,

it's never a step backward.

It's a return to your truth.

So take the first step.

Even if it's small.

Even if it's slow.

Because there is beauty in every beginning—

especially the ones you choose for yourself.

Chapter Fifty: Returning to Your True Self

Sometimes you drift so far from yourself

that you no longer recognize your own voice.

Your laughter becomes forced,

your tears fall silently,

and even the mirror no longer knows you.

But there is always a way back.

A return to a place where you wear no mask,

where you don't have to be good,

or strong,

or perfect.

Just… yourself.

Your true self may be wounded,

tired,

might even be a little broken,

but it is the most authentic version of you.

And that in itself is beautiful.

Returning to yourself means embracing all your light and your shadows.

It means letting go of comparison,

letting go of pretense,

and telling yourself this simple truth:

"You, just as you are, are enough."

This path is not easy.

Sometimes it hurts.

Sometimes it demands that you let go of things:

The roles you've played for years,

others' expectations,

even some people.

But in return, you find yourself again.

And nothing in the world is more precious than that.

Returning to yourself means coming home.

Home that has always been waiting for you—

In quiet, in patience, in love.

Chapter Fifty-One: Continuing the Journey

The end of these pages is not the end of your story.

It's simply an invitation to keep walking—

to carry these words in your heart

and let them guide you beyond these chapters.

Every day still holds questions to ask,

choices to make,

and moments that await your full presence.

The path you walk will twist and turn,

and sometimes you'll lose sight of where you began.

But remember: the real journey is not about arriving,

but about staying open to who you're becoming.

Let these pages be a companion—

a reminder that you are never truly alone

in your fears, your hopes, your doubts, or your laughter.

Your true self, the one you've been rediscovering,

is always there to walk beside you.

As you step into each new dawn,

carry forward the gentleness you've learned,

the courage that rose from your hardest days,

and the quiet power of your own voice.

Trust yourself as you have trusted these words—

and trust that life's unfolding, moment by moment,

is exactly where you're meant to be.

So close this book, and open your life.

Breathe in deeply, and step forward—

knowing that every new beginning

is born from where you stand right now.

The journey goes on, and so do you…

Chapter Fifty-Two: Gratitude – The Light That Shines in Every Moment

Sometimes you believe something grand must occur

to set your heart alight;

but gratitude is simply the tender glance

at what you already possess—a breath, a smile,

a little sun peeking behind the window.

Gratitude is the act of opening the eyes of your heart

to see that light flows even through life's highs and lows.

It's recognizing each inhale as a miracle,

each exhale as a gift.

Gratitude means standing tall

before what you have, not what you lack,

and softly saying:

"This moment right here warms my soul."

When you walk with a grateful heart,

your world transforms—

Every sound grows kinder,

every flavor tastes sweeter.

There will be days of pain,

yet even on those days,

there is something to give thanks for:

a comforting memory, a gentle hand,

a cloudy sky that nourishes the earth with rain.

Gratitude is a practice, not a fleeting feeling.

Each sunrise calls us to open our eyes

and fill our hearts with "thank you."

These little "thank you"s gather into a light

that guides you through the darkest nights—

a single candle glows

that, when all else is dark, still illuminates your path.

So today, whisper to yourself:

"Thank you for this very moment.

Thank you for every small and great blessing."

And watch how gratitude turns each moment into a celebration.

Gratitude lightens your spirit, opens your heart,

and allows life—with all its bitterness and sweetness—

to be embraced by the light that has always been here.

Chapter Fifty-Three: Purpose in Every Breath

Each breath you take is an invitation—

a reminder that life unfolds in this very moment.

Inhale deeply, and feel the world enter you;

exhale fully, and release all that no longer serves.

Purpose isn't only found in grand goals or distant dreams.

It lives in the simple rhythm of your lungs,

in the rise and fall of your chest,

in the subtle movement that keeps you tethered to now.

With every inhale, you can choose intention:

to be kinder, to open your heart,

to honor the small joys hiding in plain sight.

With every exhale, you can let go:

Of doubt, of fear, of the weight you need not carry.

When life feels chaotic, return to this breath.

Notice how it anchors you, steadying the mind,

soothing the body and guiding your steps

toward what truly matters.

Purpose in each breath means living from the inside out:

allowing your values to shape your actions,

your compassion to guide your words,

and your presence to light the path for others.

You don't need a grand sign to know your way.

Your breath is the ever-present compass,

pointing you back to your own truth,

reminding you that each moment is an opportunity

to live with intention and to love without reservation.

So breathe now—

and let each breath be both anchor and sail,

grounding you in gratitude,

and propelling you toward the life you're meant to lead.

Would you like to continue with Chapter Fifty-Four: Calm in Motion? Let me know, and we'll keep this journey going.

Chapter Fifty-Four: Calm in Motion

Calm isn't always found in stillness—

sometimes it comes through movement.

In simple steps,

in the ever-flowing current of life.

When you walk, the breeze carries your breath,

and the earth seems to dance beneath each footfall.

In that moment, you realize:

Calm is the acceptance of this very flow.

We often believe we must grip life's reins tightly

to keep everything steady.

But the truth is,

when you release that tension,

a deep calm fills the space where stress once lived.

Calm in motion means

with every step you take,

you check in with your breath:

"I am here, and I am moving."

Remember, the world is fluid—

Each morning the sun rises,

every season changes its coat,

everything is in flux.

Najiba Darwish Kakar

When you embrace this flow,

instead of resisting or fearing the unknown,

you learn to move in harmony with life.

Calm in motion means

sometimes taking just one small step,

yet doing so with faith:

"This step carries me forward."

It means opening your heart

to the unseen moments—

and knowing that

wherever you are,

that is exactly where you can feel calm.

So when you set out tomorrow,

wherever your path leads,

hold this truth close:

calm is not found in an ancient stillness,

but in every breath, every step,

shining in the very motion of living.

Chapter Fifty-Five: Light Within the Darkness

Even in the blackest night,

there is a spark waiting to be found—

a gentle glow tucked inside your soul,

ready to guide you when all else feels lost.

Darkness can feel endless,

but it is in those very shadows

that your inner light becomes most alive:

Soft, persistent, unafraid of the void.

When fear creeps close, remember this—

Your light does not compete with the dark;

it simply shines through it,

transforming shadow into space.

Each challenge you've endured

has coaxed that light forward,

teaching it to burn steady

when the world around you trembles.

Trust that even now,

as darkness swirls,

you carry a flame within you—

small but unwavering,

enough to show you home.

Chapter Fifty-Six: The Power of Hope

Hope is not loud.

It doesn't shout or demand attention.

It often whispers—

soft and steady—

In the quiet moments when you're ready to give up.

Hope is the hand that reaches out

even when everything else pulls away.

It's the voice inside that says,

"Maybe not today… but someday."

It's not blind optimism,

but a choice—

to believe in something beyond the pain,

to trust that what's heavy now won't always weigh you down.

Hope doesn't erase the dark.

It walks with you through it.

It doesn't pretend the road is easy,

but it promises:

"You won't be walking forever."

Sometimes, hope is just waking up

and deciding to try again.

Sometimes, it's allowing yourself to rest,

and knowing that rest, too, is progress.

You carry more light than you know,

and hope is what helps you find it—

again and again,

even in the middle of the storm.

So hold on to that gentle spark.

Let it guide you forward.

Because hope, quiet as it may be,

is the strength that keeps you alive.

Chapter Fifty-Seven: Returning to Yourself

You've spent so much of your life reaching outward—

for love, for safety, for meaning.

But there comes a time

when the journey must turn inward.

Returning to yourself isn't about isolation;

it's about coming home.

To your breath.

To your truth.

To the quiet voice you silenced for far too long.

You are not lost.

You are just distant from your own center—

and that center is still there,

waiting with open arms.

Coming back to yourself means

remembering who you were before the world told you who to be.

It means peeling off the layers

that were never truly yours:

the expectations, the masks, the noise.

It's not always easy.

Sometimes the silence feels strange.

Sometimes the truth feels too raw.

But stay with it.

Let the quiet hold you.

You don't have to fix everything.

You don't need all the answers.

You only need one small, honest moment

with yourself.

Because the more you return,

the more you'll see:

you were never broken.

You were just hidden beneath the weight

of everything you thought you had to carry.

And in that return,

you'll find your softness,

your strength,

your peace.

Yourself.

Fully.

Finally.

Home.

Chapter Fifty-Eight: Embracing Solitude

Solitude is not that painful, forgotten loneliness.

It is not the emptiness of someone's absence or the ache of being unseen.

It is the quiet presence of your own soul—

Finally sitting beside you, whole and unmasked.

There is a peace

That only arrives when it's just you and your breath.

No distractions,

No masks,

No need for anyone's approval.

In stillness,

You meet yourself without interruption.

You hear your thoughts,

You feel the voice of your heart.

And slowly,

You begin to remember:

You are enough, even on your own.

The world taught us to fear silence—

To fill it with noise,

To always seek connection.

But within that silence,

There is wisdom.

There is healing.

There is truth.

To embrace solitude

Is not too close your heart,

But to open it—

To yourself.

To offer the love you've freely given to others,

Now, to your own being.

Sit with yourself.

Not to escape,

But to return.

Not to be alone,

But to become whole.

Because sometimes,

The deepest connection

Is the one you quietly build

With your own soul.

Chapter Fifty-Nine: Listening to the Heart

Your heart speaks in whispers,

not in shouts.

It calls out in the quiet moments,

when everything else fades away.

It isn't always clear,

and sometimes you have to pause to hear it—

But it is always there.

Telling you what feels true,

what feels right,

what you need.

Listening to your heart isn't about finding answers all at once,

but about being willing to hear the small nudges,

the quiet guidance,

the gentle push that leads you toward yourself.

The mind can get loud.

It can flood you with doubts,

fears,

endless to-do lists.

But the heart speaks softly—

reminding you of what matters,

reminding you of your worth,

reminding you of your path.

In the noise of life,

it's easy to forget to listen.

But when you take a moment to quiet everything down,

you'll hear it.

That steady rhythm,

the pulse of your true desires.

The pulse that says:

"Here you are.

You are enough.

And you are going in the right direction."

So, trust it.

Listen to your heart's whispers,

even when the world is loud.

Let it be your guide—

not because it has all the answers,

but because it always knows

the way back to you.

Chapter Sixty: Accepting Change

Change is frightening—

Because it's unknown,

Because it takes your control,

Because you don't know what waits on the other side.

But change is part of being alive.

Every leaf that turns,

Every sunrise,

Every breath you take

Reminds you that nothing stays the same.

Sometimes we cling to the past,

Not because it was the best,

But because it was familiar.

Because familiar pain feels easier than unfamiliar hope.

But the truth is:

Growth lives in the heart of change.

Peace comes when you say,

"I don't know what's coming,

But I'm ready."

To accept change is

To let something end,

So something new can begin.

It means wiping your tears,

But continuing the path.

It means saying goodbye to what you miss,

And walking forward—with an open heart—into a tomorrow you don't yet know.

Because hidden in all this uncertainty

Are the chances

That shapes you into a newer version of yourself.

So don't be afraid.

Change may shake you,

But maybe that shake

Is exactly what you've been waiting for.

Chapter Sixty-One: Making Peace with the Past

The past doesn't disappear—

it lives in memories,

in the way your voice catches when you speak certain names,

in the quiet moments when old feelings return uninvited.

But making peace with the past

doesn't mean forgetting.

It means choosing not to let it hurt you anymore.

You are not what happened to you.

You are who you became after it.

Stronger. Softer. Wiser.

Still healing, maybe—

But still standing.

Forgiveness, especially for yourself,

isn't weakness.

It's freedom.

It's the moment you say,

"I did the best I could with what I knew then.

Now I know better. Now I choose differently."

Making peace is not a single moment.

It's a process—

a slow, gentle unfolding.

It's giving your past a place to rest,

without letting it write your future.

You can carry the lessons

without carrying the pain.

You can remember

without reliving.

You can honor who you were

and still love who you are becoming.

So take a deep breath.

Look back, not to reopen wounds,

but to thank the path that brought you here.

And then—keep walking forward.

Lightly. Freely.

At peace.

Chapter Sixty-Two: Staying Brave When There's Nothing Left

Some pain can't be spoken about.

Not because it isn't deep,

but because words fall short.

And in those moments, silence gets heavy—

not the peaceful kind,

but the kind that feels like a weight on your chest.

Still, you're here.

And that means something.

The fact that you're still breathing

means there's still a small light inside—

even if it flickers like a tired candle,

you haven't gone out.

Being brave

sometimes means sitting quietly in the dark,

until your eyes adjust,

until you start to see a path—

even a blurry one.

It means holding yourself

with the same hands that wiped away your tears last night.

It means saying:

"Today was hard…

but it's over.

And I'm still here."

That—

That is courage.

Not running.

Not shouting.

But staying.

Quietly.

With a cracked heart,

but one that still beats.

Chapter Sixty-Three: The First Light After a Long Night

It doesn't happen all at once.

The light doesn't flood in

like some grand miracle.

It seeps—

soft and slow,

like a whisper at the edge of a tired soul.

One morning,

you notice the sky isn't completely gray.

There's a hint of warmth behind the clouds.

And inside you,

something small shifts.

Not joy,

not yet.

But maybe…

relief.

Like your heart finally takes a breath

it didn't know it was holding.

This is how healing begins—

not with answers,

but with moments.

Moments where the silence doesn't hurt as much.

Where the ache becomes a hum,

and the weight in your chest feels a little lighter.

Maybe you still don't know where you're going.

But for the first time in a long time,

you feel like walking again.

And that's enough.

That's more than enough.

The first light after a long night

isn't meant to blind you—

It's meant to remind you:

You made it this far.

You can go further.

Chapter Sixty-Four: When Life Slowly Opens Again

Life is like a flower—

It doesn't bloom all at once.

Not with force,

not with urgency,

but with patience and the quiet warmth of light.

There are still dark days,

but something inside you isn't dark anymore.

There's warmth now,

a soft hope

growing slowly in your chest.

You've changed—

not through big events,

but through small choices:

to breathe,

to stay,

to keep going even when everything hurts.

And that—

That is a quiet miracle.

You've learned that joy isn't always loud.

Sometimes, it's the softest whisper that says:

"I'm still here.

And maybe, just maybe,

I'm ready to feel life again."

When you hear a bird and your heart softens a little,

when you see the sky and feel something stir—

That's life opening again.

Not like a bang,

but like a song

that begins in a hush.

And you?

You're ready to listen.

Chapter Sixty-Five: Learning to Receive the Good

You've been surviving for so long

that softness might feel unfamiliar.

Peace might feel strange.

Even happiness—

might stir something like fear in you.

Because when life has taught you

to brace for the worst,

receiving the good

can feel like waiting for it to disappear.

But listen—

Good things aren't promises to be broken.

They're gifts.

And you're allowed to hold them

without guilt,

without doubt,

without thinking you have to earn them.

You're allowed to smile

without wondering if it will cost you.

You're allowed to rest

without thinking you must first suffer.

You're allowed to feel joy

just because it showed up.

This is healing, too:

not just surviving the dark,

but allowing the light to stay.

So when life hands you something soft—

a kind word,

a quiet morning,

a moment of laughter—

Don't question it.

Just let it in.

Let it fill the places inside you

that forgot what warmth feels like.

This is not the end of the story.

This is a new kind of beginning—

gentle,

earned,

and fully yours.

Chapter Sixty-Six: Rediscovering Love for Yourself

Sometimes, the greatest challenge

is learning to love yourself.

Not out of pride,

but out of deep understanding.

That you, just like everyone else,

are worthy of love—

Love that needs no reason.

Be kind to yourself.

Be patient with yourself.

Make time for yourself,

because you, too, are human,

with all your wounds and flaws.

Learn to forgive yourself.

Learn to see yourself,

not through the lens of mistakes,

but through the eyes of hope.

Through the eyes of someone who still holds something alive within them—

even if it's small,

but full of potential for a new beginning.

Loving yourself means knowing

you deserve peace and happiness.

It means that even when the world feels cold,

you can still rebuild it

with the warmth inside you.

And when you learn to love yourself,

loving others becomes more natural.

Because from yourself, you learn how to

embrace others with compassion, with kindness,

with all that you are.

Loving yourself,

isn't about arrogance,

but about accepting yourself as you are—

And that is the greatest gift you can give yourself.

Chapter Sixty-Seven: The Courage to Begin Again

Sometimes, starting over feels like a mountain you're not sure you can climb.

The weight of past failures, past fears,

they can hold you back,

make you question if you're strong enough to take the first step.

But here's the thing:

You don't have to carry everything at once.

You don't need to have the whole journey figured out.

All you need is the courage to take one step forward.

Starting over isn't a sign of weakness—

It's a sign of strength.

It takes immense courage to say,

"I'm ready for something new,"

even when the past feels heavy.

You are allowed to begin again.

You are allowed to leave behind what no longer serves you—

and take with you the lessons,

the growth,

the wisdom that has shaped you.

Every new beginning,

no matter how small,

It is a victory.

And with each step,

You become more of who you are meant to be.

So, when the road ahead seems uncertain,

Don't be afraid.

Trust yourself.

Because the act of starting again

It is the act of living.

Chapter Sixty-Eight: Embracing Fear, but with Hope

Fear isn't always a bad thing.

Sometimes, fear is a sign that you're moving toward something bigger.

Those moments when your heart shakes,

when your steps slow down,

are the moments when you're growing.

When fear comes,

you might feel like you can't move forward,

but in truth, that's where you can take a new step for yourself.

Because fear is simply the way that says,

"This is the place where you need to push harder."

Fear can walk with you,

but you have to decide to let it stay as a companion, not let it define your path.

Embracing fear means finding the strength

to face it.

Learn to find hope within fear.

Learn to move forward without any guarantees.

Learn to take courageous steps even when your heart is filled with doubt.

Yes, you might face fear on the way,

but that fear will teach you that you are stronger than you thought.

You have the power to move through the shadows of fear

and reach the light—

even when you still don't know how.

This new beginning may not always come with certainty,

But those hesitant steps will take you to a place

that one day, you will be proud of.

Chapter Seventy: Finding Peace amid the Storm

Sometimes, life feels like a storm.

The events around you

are like fierce winds and relentless rain,

leaving you little room for peace.

But here's the truth:

Peace is always somewhere we choose to find it,

not out there, but inside ourselves.

The world might be filled with chaos,

but within your heart,

you can find a place

that no storm can touch.

Peace doesn't come from removing problems,

but from learning how to deal with them.

Sometimes, when you want to control everything,

you simply have to let it come and go—

without holding onto it.

This is acceptance—

accepting that life isn't always in our control,

yet still knowing you can move forward

with trust in yourself, no matter what the circumstances.

Peace comes when you realize:

"Even in this storm, I am here.

I am still standing.

And no matter what, I will keep moving forward."

I hope this chapter brings some peace into your heart.

Chapter Seventy-One: When You Don't Know What You Want, but You Keep Going

Sometimes, nothing is clear.

Not your wants,

not your direction,

not even the reason why you're still moving forward.

But still, you go.

With shaky steps,

With a heart full of questions,

Yet still beating, refusing to stop.

Sometimes, life is like that—

not filled with certainty,

but with a quiet hope that flickers in the dark.

A hope that whispers:

"Not everything makes sense, but maybe the path will show itself…

if you just take one more step."

You don't have to understand everything.

You don't have to feel everything clearly.

You only need to listen to that small voice inside that says,

"Keep going."

Because so often,

meaning finds you along the way—

Not before you begin.

And you,

With all your uncertainty and doubt,

You're still living.

And that, in itself,

It is something beautiful.

Chapter Seventy-Two: Learning to Rest Without Guilt

You're allowed to pause.

You're allowed to breathe.

You're allowed to rest—

not because you're weak,

But because you're human.

In a world that glorifies hustle,

pushing forward no matter the cost,

The rest feels like rebellion.

But it's not.

It's necessary.

It's healing.

It's a quiet way of saying,

"My worth is not measured by how much I produce."

Rest is not quitting.

It's a gentle reset.

A moment to gather strength,

to soften the edges of exhaustion,

to remind yourself that you are not a machine.

Let the stillness hold you.

Let the silence speak.

Let the softness in you rise again

without apology.

Because even the strongest hearts need rest,

Even the brightest flames need to dim sometimes

to burn again, brighter.

You deserve that rest.

And when you return—

You'll rise with more clarity,

more purpose,

more peace.

Chapter Seventy-Three: Slowly Returning to Yourself

After a long stretch of exhaustion,

After days, you just wanted to survive,

coming back to yourself

feels like waking from a deep, heavy sleep.

Not in a rush.

Not with pressure.

But with a soft breath,

a kind glance in the mirror,

and a small smile—

maybe not fully real yet,

but real enough to begin.

You find yourself again

not by getting answers from the world,

But by listening to that quiet voice inside.

The one that's always been there,

just buried beneath the world's noise.

You learn to walk gently.

To not fear the silence.

To know that even when "motivation" is missing,

You are still here—

still you—

And that is enough.

Coming back might not be easy.

Some days may still feel dark.

But now, you know:

even in the darkness,

There's a light within you.

That doesn't fade.

And that—

That is a new beginning.

Chapter Seventy-Four: The Gentle Power of Starting Small

Healing doesn't always come in grand moments.

It doesn't shout or arrive with a dramatic sunrise.

Sometimes,

healing looks like getting out of bed.

Drinking water.

Opening the window.

Answering a message.

Taking a shower.

These small things—

They matter.

They are the quiet victories

that no one claps for,

But they count.

You don't need to rebuild your life in one day.

You don't have to leap forward with clarity and confidence.

You only need to take one step,

and then another,

no matter how small,

no matter how slow.

There is power in the tiniest beginnings.

There is strength in showing up,

especially on the days when everything feels heavy.

Celebrate the little things.

They are not little at all.

They are proof that you're trying,

that you're here,

That you haven't given up.

And that—

That is everything.

Chapter Seventy-Five: Being Kind to Yourself—Even When You Don't Know How

Some days, nothing feels right.

Your heart is heavy,

Your mind is tired,

And you don't even know why the weight is still there.

But on those days,

The most powerful thing you can do

It is to be gentle with yourself.

Not because everything is okay,

But because you still deserve softness—

even when you can't see the reason.

Being kind to yourself

means speaking to yourself like someone you love.

It means not criticizing your every move,

But offering a quiet comfort instead,

When all you need

It is to feel held, not judged.

Sometimes, you are your own safest place.

Not someone else.

Not a quick solution.

Just your quiet presence—

An invisible hug

In the middle of all the noise.

And from that place,

Healing begins.

Not with a big change,

But with a small moment of kindness.

That small kindness

It is the first step back to yourself—

and to a life built with care,

not chaos.

Chapter Seventy-Six: You Don't Have to Rush Your Healing

There's no timeline for feeling okay again.

No deadline for when the sadness should lift,

Or when the energy should return.

Some days will feel light.

Others, heavy.

And that's not failure—

That's healing.

Healing is not a straight road.

It twists, turns, doubles back,

pauses.

It doesn't care for calendars or expectations.

So if you're still not okay today,

That's okay.

You're allowed to move slowly.

You're allowed to take breaks.

You're allowed to simply breathe—

And call that enough.

Your worth is not tied to your progress.

Your value is not measured by your productivity.

You are not behind.

You are right where you need to be—

even if you can't see it yet.

Trust that your pace is your own.

Gentle.

True.

And just right for you.

Chapter Seventy-Seven: Quiet Strength

There is a kind of strength.

That doesn't roar.

It doesn't stand on stages,

doesn't need to be seen,

doesn't beg to be applauded.

It lives quietly—

In the way you keep showing up,

even when you're tired.

In the way you get back up,

even after falling again and again.

In the way you hold space for your pain

without letting it become all that you are.

This strength

It is softer than what the world usually celebrates—

But it runs deeper.

It's in your ability to feel everything

and still choose to love,

to hope,

to try.

You don't have to be loud to be powerful.

You don't have to be fearless to be brave.

You don't have to be perfect to be enough.

The quiet strength in you—

It's real.

It's growing.

And it's already carrying you

further than you think

Chapter Seventy-Eight: Finding Joy in the Small Things

Joy isn't always found in the big moments.

Sometimes, it's in a warm cup of tea,

The sunlight resting gently on your hands,

Or a song that quietly reminds you of a sweet memory.

Sometimes joy

is simply taking a deep breath

And realizing today feels just a little lighter than yesterday.

Or laughing without meaning to—

for no reason at all.

You don't have to feel joyful all the time,

But you can learn to notice joy,

even in the tiniest places.

In the middle of exhaustion,

In ordinary days,

In the things that used to pass you by—

until you stopped and felt them.

Life isn't always made of grand things.

Often, it's the small joys

that keep you going.

And you—

You deserve those moments.

You deserve to smile,

even if the reason is small,

even if it doesn't last long.

Chapter Seventy-Nine: The Pain That Softened You

No one walks through life untouched by pain.

Behind every smile,

There's a story,

a quiet ache,

a night spent wide awake with thoughts too heavy to carry.

But not all pain is meant to break you.

Some pain—

It softened you.

It taught you how to listen.

How to sit beside someone else's sorrow and not try to fix it,

just to be there.

It taught you that tears are not weakness,

But a sign that your heart still feels deeply.

That asking for help is not giving up—

It's choosing to keep going,

together.

Some pain leads you inward,

where strength doesn't roar

But hums quietly in the way you keep showing up,

In the way you continue to love

even with a tender, healing heart.

And now,

Because of everything you've walked through,

you understand people a little more.

You judge a little less.

You love a little deeper.

The pain didn't just leave you wounded.

It left you wiser.

Softer.

And more alive.

Chapter Eighty: Finding Joy in the Small Things

Joy isn't always found in the big moments.

Sometimes, it's in a warm cup of tea,

The sunlight resting gently on your hands,

Or a song that quietly reminds you of a sweet memory.

Sometimes joy

is simply taking a deep breath

And realizing today feels just a little lighter than yesterday.

Or laughing without meaning to—

for no reason at all.

You don't have to feel joyful all the time,

But you can learn to notice joy,

even in the tiniest places.

In the middle of exhaustion,

In ordinary days,

In the things that used to pass you by—

until you stopped and felt them.

Life isn't always made of grand things.

Often, it's the small joys

that keep you going.

And you—

You deserve those moments.

You deserve to smile,

even if the reason is small,

even if it doesn't last long.

Chapter Eighty-One: The Freedom in Letting Go

Sometimes, holding on feels like the only choice.

We cling to what we know,

to what we think we can control,

to old stories,

to things that no longer serve us,

But have become a part of who we are.

But freedom comes when we let go.

It's not forgetting the past,

It's not erasing the pain.

It's simply choosing to release the weight you no longer need to carry.

Choosing to step out of the shadows of yesterday

and into the light of today.

Letting go doesn't mean you're weak.

It means you're strong enough to trust that your future will be more than the remnants of the past.

It means having the courage to create space in your heart for new experiences,

new people,

and new beginnings.

When you let go,

You allow yourself to breathe freely again.

You make room for hope,

for peace,

And for all the things that life has to offer you.

The past has shaped you,

But it doesn't have to define you forever.

The freedom is in the choice to move forward,

to live,

to love,

to grow.

Chapter Eighty-Two: Self-Forgiveness: A Gift to the Heart

Sometimes, the hardest thing to forgive is ourselves.

We are often our harshest critics,

carrying the weight of past mistakes,

feeling like those errors still follow us with every step we take.

But part of growth is learning how to forgive ourselves.

Not because everything is perfect,

but because we understand that making mistakes is part of being human.

We can't escape our errors,

but we can choose to see them as teachers,

offering lessons we needed to learn.

Self-forgiveness doesn't mean ignoring our mistakes.

It means accepting that we aren't perfect,

and that imperfection is what makes us human.

It's recognizing that along the way,

we've lost our way,

but we're still learning, still growing.

This forgiveness isn't weakness,

It's a sign of strength.

It's the courage to accept ourselves,

With all our flaws and failures,

and to keep moving forward.

You have the right to forgive yourself.

You have the right to stop living in the past,

and to permit yourself to step into the future

With a lighter heart,

and a freer mind.

Chapter Eighty-Three: Embracing Self-Acceptance and Inner Peace

True peace begins the moment we accept ourselves as we are.

Not as we wish we were,

not as we think we should be,

But as we truly are, with all our imperfections,

all our scars,

and all the beautiful, messy parts of us that make us human.

Self-acceptance is the key to unlocking inner peace.

It's the understanding that we don't have to be perfect to be worthy.

We don't need to have it all together to deserve love.

We are enough, just as we are.

This doesn't mean we stop growing or striving to be better.

It means we release the constant pressure to be flawless.

We stop chasing an unrealistic version of ourselves

and instead, we embrace the person we are right now.

We honor our journey, our struggles,

and all the lessons that have shaped us.

When we accept ourselves,

We stop fighting against our flaws,

And we begin to flow with life,

allowing ourselves the grace to make mistakes,

the patience to heal,

and the love to keep moving forward.

Inner peace isn't a distant goal—

It's the gift we give ourselves the moment we stop resisting.

It's the calm we find when we stop looking for approval

and start listening to our hearts.

You deserve peace.

You deserve to feel whole,

And you deserve to embrace the person you've become,

Exactly as you are.

Chapter Eighty-Four: Nurturing Inner Peace, Even in Hard Times

Inner peace doesn't only arrive when life is easy.

Sometimes, it shows up when everything around you feels heavy,

when your mind is loud

and your heart is tired.

That's exactly when peace becomes the most needed.

But peace doesn't come from outside.

Not from people,

not from perfect circumstances,

not from everything being "fixed."

Peace is a choice—

a quiet decision you make within yourself.

Learn to breathe deeply in the middle of the storm.

Learn to pause in the noise,

to take a moment that belongs only to you—

even if it's just by closing your eyes and saying to yourself:

"I accept this moment, just as it is."

Sometimes, you don't need to fix everything.

You just need to permit yourself to be.

Exactly as you are, exactly where you are.

Peace is about finding a safe space inside yourself.

It's about holding on to hope, even when fear is present.

It's knowing that life is always changing—

And you can move with the waves,

not fight against them.

Even on the darkest days,

You still hold the power to create light—

from within.

Chapter Eighty-Five: Being Gentle with Your Fears

Fear isn't always loud—

Sometimes, it's quiet.

A whisper in the back of your mind,

a hesitation in your step,

a tightness in your chest when something unknown appears.

And the truth is,

fear is not your enemy.

It's a part of you that's trying to protect you,

even if it doesn't always know how.

Being gentle with your fears means

not pushing them away,

not pretending they don't exist,

But meeting them with compassion.

Sitting beside your fear like you would with a scared child,

offering comfort instead of shame.

Ask yourself:

What is this fear trying to tell me?

What part of me feels unsafe, unseen, or uncertain?

When you stop running from your fears,

you give yourself a chance to understand them.

And in understanding them,

they lose some of their power.

Courage doesn't mean you're never afraid.

It means you keep walking anyway—

with your fear beside you,

but not in control.

So be gentle.

Breathe with your fear.

Speak kindly to the parts of you that tremble.

Because healing doesn't always roar.

Sometimes, it sounds like a whisper that says,

"I'm scared… but I'm still here."

Chapter Eighty-Six: Rebuilding Yourself After Pain and Heartbreak

When your heart breaks,

when life doesn't go the way you hoped,

when it feels like something you loved is gone forever—

That's when rebuilding begins.

Rebuilding means finding yourself again.

Not becoming who you were before,

but creating a deeper, calmer, wiser version of yourself.

Someone who has scars,

but is still standing.

Someone who has cried,

but now sees life through eyes filled with experience.

Pain is never simple.

But inside pain,

there is something that can shape you into someone stronger.

Every heartbreak,

every disappointment,

every time you whispered, "I can't do this anymore,"

was secretly teaching you how to say, "I still can."

Rebuilding takes time.

Step by step.

Some days you'll feel progress,

And some days, just breathing will be a victory.

Give yourself that time.

Let your heart slowly begin to believe again.

You are not just a survivor of your pain—

You are someone who, even in ruins,

planted seeds for something new.

Chapter Eighty-Seven: Growing Hope from the Ashes

Hope doesn't always arrive with bright light.

Sometimes, it starts as a quiet flicker—

a tiny warmth in the cold,

a whisper in the silence of your sorrow.

After everything falls apart,

After you've sat in the ashes of what used to be,

There comes a moment—

gentle, almost invisible—

When your heart dares to wonder:

"Maybe things can be good again."

This is where hope is born.

Not from forcing yourself to "move on,"

But from letting life return slowly.

From allowing tiny moments of joy to matter again.

From smiling at a morning breeze,

feeling comfort in a kind word,

or simply getting through the day.

Hope grows in the cracks—

In the places you thought were too broken.

And day by day, without rush,

You begin to believe again.

You don't need to have it all figured out.

You don't need to pretend you're not hurting.

All you need is the courage to keep showing up—

to keep breathing,

to keep hoping,

even when it's hard.

Because one day, you'll look back

And see how far you've come.

How from all that burn down?

Something beautiful began to grow.

Chapter Eighty-Eight: Letting Your Heart Open to Joy—Even When There's Still Pain

Joy doesn't always come after the pain is gone.

Sometimes, it arrives quietly,

sitting beside your tears,

showing up when you least expect it.

You might believe you need to be "fully healed" first—

That your wounds need to be closed

before you're allowed to smile again.

But life doesn't work that way.

Joy doesn't wait for perfection.

It comes in the middle of your healing,

In the quiet spaces of tired days,

in small, unexpected moments

That reminds you: you're still alive.

Letting your heart open to joy

means allowing both happiness and hurt to exist side by side.

It means permitting yourself to laugh,

even when part of you still aches.

It means knowing you don't have to "earn" joy—

You simply have to allow it.

Joy is like sunlight—

even if you open the window just a little,

It will find its way in.

Learn to live with your pain,

But don't close yourself off to life's sweetness.

Light candles in your darkness,

even if they're small,

even if they flicker.

Joy is a choice,

not because everything is perfect,

But because you are worthy of it—

Right now, just as you are.

Chapter Eighty-Nine: Trusting Again After Loss

Trust is delicate.

When it's broken, it can feel like a crack in the foundation of your life.

You might wonder if you'll ever be able to rebuild it,

if you'll ever trust again.

But here's the truth:

Trust is not something you either have or don't.

It's something you grow slowly,

like planting seeds and waiting for them to sprout.

After a loss, it's natural to feel guarded.

To want to protect your heart,

to keep it safe from more pain.

But if you keep the door locked forever,

you'll miss the beauty that can come from trust.

Trusting again doesn't mean forgetting what happened,

Or pretending the hurt isn't real.

It means understanding that, despite your past,

there is still room in your heart to believe again.

It means permitting yourself to be vulnerable,

even if it feels risky.

Start small.

Trust a friend with a little piece of yourself.

Trust that things can improve, one step at a time.

Trust that you are strong enough to handle whatever comes next.

And most importantly, trust yourself.

You are capable of loving again.

You are capable of healing.

You are capable of moving forward, even if it's with a heart that has known loss.

Chapter Ninety: Building a Life with Purpose and Clarity

Life is not always simple.

But within the complexities, there's always a path you can find.

This path is one of purpose and clarity.

Sometimes, amidst the hustle and bustle of everyday life, we forget what truly matters to us.

We get caught up in duties, desires, and expectations,

and often forget where we want to go.

Building a life with purpose means having a roadmap for each day.

It means lighting a lantern that shows you where your true goals lie,

even when the outside world feels dark.

On this path, it doesn't matter how many times you go astray or stray from your course.

What matters is that you always return to your path.

Each day is an opportunity to step closer to what you wish to build.

Clarity in life means knowing yourself,

understanding what truly matters, and what doesn't.

Clarity means learning from your experiences

and always keeping your eyes on the horizon, even when you don't know where the next step will lead.

Learn to guide your life toward what you truly believe in.

Learn that every decision you make should be a step toward building your life with purpose.

This may not always be easy,

But when you live with purpose,

Each day takes on its meaning.

Chapter Ninety-One: Embracing New Beginnings and the Opportunities Within Change

New beginnings are often disguised as endings.

They come when you least expect them,

After a chapter has closed,

leaving you standing on the edge of uncertainty.

But here's the truth:

Change is the soil in which growth takes root.

Without it, we remain stagnant,

trapped in the comfort of what's familiar,

even if it no longer serves us.

Embracing new beginnings means letting go of the old

and trusting that the unknown can lead to something better.

It's about accepting that, sometimes, the end of one thing is the birth of another.

The fear of change is natural.

But the beauty of it is that it brings opportunities—

new lessons, new perspectives,

and new chances to become who we are meant to be.

Start small.

A new habit, a new hobby, a new way of thinking.

Every small step forward is a new beginning.

Even if you don't know where it's leading,

Trust that it's part of your journey.

Embrace the discomfort that change often brings,

because it's in those moments of discomfort that you discover your true strength.

It's when you step into the unknown that you realize how much more you are capable of.

New beginnings don't always come with a clear map,

But they are always filled with potential.

And with every new beginning, you have the power to create something meaningful.

Chapter Ninety-Two: Finding Peace amid Uncertainty

Life is often filled with uncertainty.

We search for stability and security,

But naturally, life is ever-changing.

When we don't know what the future holds,

when paths become unclear,

it's easy to feel like we're out of control.

But true peace comes when we learn to find calm within this uncertainty.

Peace amidst change means learning how

to flow with life's changes

and allow them to help us grow.

It means accepting that some things are beyond our control

and realizing that, in those moments,

We can discover our inner strength.

Every change or uncertainty is an opportunity for growth.

If you've been able to navigate difficult times in the past,

you can face changes and the unknown with confidence.

Peace in uncertainty means allowing yourself to breathe,

to accept new paths, even if they lead you to unknown places.

It means trusting that even when the way is unclear,

your steps will take you to something worthwhile.

In these times of uncertainty,

learn to embrace life as it is,

and know that change will always be in your favor,

even if you don't fully understand it at first.

Peace doesn't come from the absence of problems,

But from learning how to face them.

Learn to find your own space amidst life's complexities,

and use it to keep moving forward.

Chapter Ninety-Three: Nurturing Growth During Times of Change

Times of change are always filled with both challenges and opportunities.

Sometimes, changes can feel like they are shaking everything up,

but deep within them, the seeds of growth are being planted.

Nurturing growth during times of change means learning

how to use every moment of change to your advantage.

These moments are opportunities to learn more,

to discover yourself, and to experience inner transformation.

In such times, you may feel like everything is falling apart,

But the truth is, when everything breaks down,

It creates space for rebuilding and becoming better.

Small, steady steps help you move forward during these times.

These changes teach you that there is always something new to find—

a new path, a new strength, a new perspective.

Every day is a new opportunity to grow.

The circumstances may have changed,

But you still have the power to find opportunities within them.

Learn to face changes, not with fear, but with courage.

These changes won't take you from one place to another;

they will transform you into a better version of yourself.

Nurturing growth during these times means seeing every change as a teacher.

Every challenge you face is a new lesson,

and every doubt you feel is an opportunity to discover your inner strength.

Chapter Ninety-Four: Building Courage in the Face of Challenges

Courage is not the absence of fear, but the ability to move forward despite it.

It's natural to feel fear when facing challenges—

whether they're big or small.

But the real measure of courage is not whether or not you feel fear,

but whether or not you act in spite of it.

When challenges arise, it's easy to shrink back,

to question your ability,

or to doubt whether you can overcome what's ahead.

But courage is found when you push through those doubts,

step by step, even when you're unsure of the outcome.

Building courage requires practice.

It means showing up for yourself every single day,

even when you feel vulnerable,

and facing what scares you with a steady heart.

Start small—take that first step, even if it feels terrifying.

Each time you face a fear, you build a little more courage,

and with each small victory, your confidence grows.

Remember, courage isn't about being fearless—

it's about knowing fear is there,

and choosing to move forward anyway.

It's the quiet voice inside you that says,

"Keep going, even when the road is tough."

The challenges you face are not obstacles to avoid,

but opportunities to develop strength.

With each challenge, you learn more about yourself,

about your resilience, and about your ability to keep moving forward.

In the end, courage isn't about the absence of fear,

but about having the strength to face it.

And with every challenge you overcome,

you are becoming the person you are meant to be.

Chapter Ninety-Five: Turning Fear into Fuel for Growth

Fear is one of the most powerful human emotions.

At times, fear can stop us,

hold us back, and make us hesitate.

But the truth is, fear can become fuel for growth

if we learn how to face it.

When managed correctly, fear can show us where

We need to push harder,

where we need to explore more,

And where we need to show more courage.

When we encounter fear, our first reaction is often to run away from it.

But if we pause for a moment and pay attention to it,

We can see that fear usually has a message for us—

a message about a new place we need to step into,

or a part of ourselves we need to embrace courageously.

Turning fear into fuel for growth means

using it as a guide, not a barrier.

Every time we encounter fear,

we can view it as a sign that new opportunities are ahead.

Opportunities to discover courage and untapped potential within ourselves.

Fear, in itself, cannot stop us,

but when we run from it, we lose the chance to grow.

If we choose to face it instead of avoid it,

we are moving closer to becoming a better version of ourselves.

Learn to see fear not as an enemy,

but as part of your journey.

With every step you take in the face of fear,

you become more aware, stronger, and braver.

Chapter Ninety-Six: Embracing Challenges as Opportunities for Progress

Challenges are an inevitable part of life, and often,

we view them as obstacles that stand in the way of our goals.

But what if we shifted our perspective and saw challenges as opportunities for progress?

What if we embraced them as essential stepping stones on our journey to growth?

Every challenge presents a chance to develop a new skill,

to strengthen our resilience, and to expand our capacity for overcoming adversity.

Rather than seeing challenges as something to avoid,

we can learn to approach them with curiosity and openness.

When we face a challenge, we are given the opportunity to learn more about ourselves—

to uncover strengths we didn't know we had,

to discover creative solutions, and to build the confidence needed to tackle future challenges.

Embracing challenges doesn't mean making things easier for ourselves;

It means choosing to step into discomfort and uncertainty with courage,

knowing that growth happens in those moments of discomfort.

Challenges are the catalysts for transformation.

They push us out of our comfort zones and into a space where we can become more than we were before.

It is through overcoming challenges that we realize our true potential.

Every challenge, no matter how difficult, is a chance to become stronger, wiser, and more resilient.

The obstacles that once seemed insurmountable can become the very experiences that shape our character and define our success.

So, when you face a challenge, instead of seeing it as a roadblock,

ask yourself: "What is this challenge teaching me?

How can I grow from this experience?

What opportunities does this challenge bring into my life?"

Chapter Ninety-Seven: Maintaining a Positive Mindset During Difficult Times

Life is often full of challenges and obstacles,

and in these times, we may sometimes feel like we've lost the strength to cope with our problems.

But in these tough moments, one of the most important things that can help us

is maintaining a positive mindset.

A positive mindset doesn't mean denying problems or forcing happiness at all costs,

But rather, it means looking for opportunities within the struggles.

When we face difficulties, our first reaction may be negative,

But if we learn to view these problems as lessons and opportunities for growth,

We can strengthen our positive outlook.

Maintaining a positive mindset during difficult times means

believing that we can still overcome these challenges,

even when we don't have all the answers yet.

It's about having faith in ourselves and trusting that we can move through the hardships.

One important way to maintain a positive mindset is by remembering what we have and being grateful for it.

Sometimes, amidst the struggles, we forget that our lives are full of blessings and valuable opportunities.

Reminding ourselves of these things can help us focus less on what we lack and more on what we have,

giving us the strength to move forward.

Also, don't forget the importance of human connection.

Sometimes, the best way to maintain a positive mindset during difficult times

is by talking to loved ones, friends, or those who inspire us.

These connections remind us that we are not alone and that we can move forward together.

Remember, having a positive mindset doesn't mean accepting everything easily.

There are times when, to maintain inner peace, we need to allow ourselves to express our feelings,

but afterward, we must remember that we still have the power to get through it.

Life is full of ups and downs, but what keeps us going is

The positive mindset and belief in ourselves, which helps us discover new ways to grow even in the toughest times.

Chapter Ninety-Eight: Rebuilding Confidence After Setbacks

There are times in life when we face setbacks—moments when things don't go as planned,

When we fall short of our expectations, or when we experience failure.

During these times, it's easy to lose confidence and question our abilities.

But the truth is, setbacks are not the end of the journey; they are part of it.

Rebuilding confidence after a setback starts with acknowledging the feeling of disappointment or failure,

But not allowing it to define who we are.

It's important to remember that failure is not a reflection of our worth,

But a moment in time where we learn, grow, and adjust.

The first step in rebuilding confidence is to practice self-compassion.

Instead of being hard on ourselves for making mistakes, we need to treat ourselves with kindness and understanding.

Recognize that everyone experiences setbacks, and it's okay to stumble along the way.

What matters is how we rise and keep moving forward.

Next, we need to reflect on what the setback has taught us.

Every failure or disappointment holds a lesson,

and those lessons are the building blocks for future success.

By embracing what we've learned, we can take those insights and apply them to our next steps.

Another important step is to focus on small victories.

When confidence is shaken, it's crucial to celebrate even the smallest progress.

Every little achievement, no matter how minor it may seem, is a reminder that we are capable and resilient.

These small wins add up over time and help restore our belief in ourselves.

Rebuilding confidence also requires us to set new, realistic goals.

Sometimes, a setback can make our dreams feel distant,

but by setting manageable goals and taking incremental steps, we can rebuild momentum.

The key is to focus on progress, not perfection.

Lastly, surround yourself with positive influences.

Being around supportive friends, mentors, or people who uplift you can make a significant difference in restoring confidence.

They remind us of our strengths, encourage us to keep going, and help us see beyond the setback.

Remember, confidence is not something that is lost permanently.

It can be rebuilt, strengthened, and refined through perseverance and self-belief.

A setback is not the end; it's simply an opportunity to start again with greater wisdom and resilience.

Chapter Ninety-Nine: A Resilient Mindset – The Key to Lasting Progress

Sometimes, life doesn't change quickly—it moves slowly, with quiet steps.

Results don't show up overnight,

and the journey toward our goals feels more like a marathon than a sprint.

In these moments, what keeps us going isn't just motivation—

It's resilience.

A mindset that says,

"Even if it's hard right now, if I keep going, I will get there."

A resilient mindset means understanding that growth takes time,

And that mistakes are a natural part of the path.

It means that when you fall, instead of giving up, you whisper to yourself:

"It's okay. I'll rise again."

Resilience is about not chasing instant results—

But focusing instead on daily efforts,

on those small, steady steps that eventually build big changes.

The most successful people aren't always the strongest or the smartest,

But they are the ones who keep going.

They've learned how to hold on to hope,

even in the face of doubt.

And the good news?

Resilience can be built with practice.

It starts when you ask yourself,

"What small step can I take today that brings me closer to my goal?"

And on the days you feel tired, you gently remind yourself why you began.

No success story exists without moments of exhaustion, doubt, or discouragement.

But the one who keeps going through all of it—

That's the one who sees the breakthrough.

Remember, resilience isn't just about trying harder—

It's about believing in yourself,

respecting your process,

and accepting that real growth takes time.

You can go slowly.

You can make mistakes.

But as long as you don't quit,

You are still on your way.

Chapter One Hundred: Letting Go of Expectations and Unfair Comparisons

These days, life's full of voices telling you:

"Look at that person—how far they've gone."

"You should've been there by now."

"You're not enough. Try harder."

And those voices?

They start to wear you down.

Little by little, you find yourself comparing.

To people you barely know—

To their polished photos, their highlight reels.

And soon, you start doubting your path.

But here's the real thing—

You're already enough.

Exactly as you are.

You don't need to be like anyone else to be valuable.

Your journey looks different, and that's what makes it beautiful.

When you carry heavy expectations,

When you keep measuring yourself against someone else's timeline,

You lose your joy.

You lose your peace.

And worst of all, you lose trust in your rhythm.

But when you drop all of that—

When you let go of the pressure, the rush, the need to "catch up"—

Something soft happens.

You breathe easier.

You start to feel lighter.

And your heart?

It begins to trust the process again.

Be you.

Move at your pace.

And remind yourself—

You don't need to prove anything to anyone.

Maybe your growth is quiet.

Maybe it's slow.

But it's steady.

And one day, you'll look back and be so proud

of how far you've come,

simply by not giving up.

So let go of the weight.

Let go of unfair comparisons.

And let life unfold on your terms.

Paradox for "The Mirror of Life" by Najiba Darwish

The book The Mirror of Life by Najiba Darwish emerges as a journey into the heart of human contradictions and paradoxes, a space where wounds and deep pains are spoken of, yet hope and restoration are equally emphasized. Najiba Darwish discusses the inner disharmony of individuals and how, at times, life weighs us down, while at other times, a simple smile plants a new seed of hope in our hearts.

The book may seem simple on the surface, but it deeply challenges the most profound human questions. In a place where the author speaks of "silence" as a refuge for silent pains, they discuss human emotions in all their dimensions: courage and weakness, hope and despair, freedom and bondage within love.

The paradox and contradiction in this book are not just found in its words, but in the essence of its message. On one hand, Najiba Darwish speaks of pain and failure, while on the other, she places hope and life alongside it. In between, "hiding" from life is not about escaping it but finding a sanctuary within oneself for healing and moving forward.

In reality, The Mirror of Life shows that anyone searching for peace within themselves not only suffers from pain but is also in the process of transformation. That with every moment we endure pain, we discover new strengths within ourselves, and this paradox is inherently embedded in our growth process. This book is for those who find themselves between pain and hope, seeking clearer paths for their lives.

The central paradox of this book lies in confronting human dualities: while it speaks of endless wounds and pains, it simultaneously invites the reader to embrace hope and change. The book is not only a space for pain but also an opportunity to emerge from it. It reveals how life, from the depths of darkness, finds its light, and how every wound becomes an opportunity for growth.

The Mirror of Life, as a reflection of real lives, reminds the reader that even in moments when we feel left behind by the world, we still have the power to stand up and continue.